Mor‗

*Taking the Serious
Out of Sports*

Bill Rogan

MaxQ Enterprises, L.L.C.
A Rocky Mountain Publisher
www.maxq4u.com

Printed and bound in the United States of America.

ISBN 978-0-9796238-4-4
Cover Photo by Linda Lee
Sketches by Brian Blaise
www.briansblaise.com

Cover Characters: Bill Rogan, himself; Casey Bloyer,
golfer; Brett Davis, baseball player; Andy Cornell, boxer;
Don Apodaca, football coach; Anné Cornell, runner; Amber
Marcelli, hockey goalie; Martin Higgins, tuba player; Justin
Adams, head coming out of tuba.

Foreword

When I was approached to write the foreword to More Turf Tales, my first thought was, "Did I miss *Less* Turf Tales?" The truth is, I loved the original Turf Tales book. Much the same way a mother loves an unplanned child; forced upon her, but the love grows over time. Now, in all seriousness, I believe More Turf Tales to be one of Bill's finest works. And having known his work I can say the bar was not set high. It's like the Yankees beating the Hudson Valley Renegades 25–2; a sure victory, but one you don't go bragging to mom about.

For 6 years I have co–hosted Artificial Turf, "America's most beloved sports talk show." In those six years I have been exposed to the mind of Bill Rogan— creative, funny, and yet mildly crazy. But as my oldest sister taught me, "crazy beats strong." From across the Denver Airwaves to business, and as a reliable friend, Bill always proves himself to be a top–notch guy. His witty, sarcastic, and at times, offensive humor is truly unmatched.

More Turf Tales is a hilarious and timeless book to add to any and all sports enthusiast's collection. Beyond sports fans, anybody seeking a good laugh will love it. It's a book you can grab off the coffee table, or back of the toilet, read a few tales, and create a gut–busting good time! This book should not be given to your great uncle with a weak bladder, unless the appropriate clean–up precautions have been made.

There is no denying that Bill's true passion is baseball. Shortly after I started on the Artificial Turf program, Bill dropped one of my all–time favorite one– liners, "Andy there's only two things that keep me out of the Majors—talent and ability." While those two factors may have been absent in his baseball skills, they are not missing in his writing or broadcasting career. Bill's memory of facts, uncanny knowledge of stats, unique insight, and unmatched humor allow him to deliver a masterpiece like More Turf Tales.

In the midst of a poor economy and difficult times in America today, More Turf Tales is the book your family and friends need to lighten their mood and enjoy a laugh at someone else's expense—the best kind of laugh to have.

No matter if you are an obsessed baseball junkie, a fanatic football freak, or a casual sports fan, More Turf Tales appeals to all readers, so you are sure to find a favorite story. Whether you LIKE More Turf Tales or LOVE it, one thing is certain—you will never read another book like!

Enjoy.

Coach Andrew Cornell

Table of Contents

RESCUED

Washington Nationals pitcher Tyler Clippard has been found alive and well, although shaken, after being lost for two days in the Coors Field Forest behind the center field wall.

"I just went from our bullpen into the forest to retrieve a Carlos Gonzalez home run ball," explained Clippard. "But I couldn't find the ball and then I got lost and panicked."

Rockies General Manager Dan O'Dowd said, "We always brief the opposing team that venturing away from the bullpen towards the trees and fountains in center field isn't a wise idea. Unfortunately, Clippard found out the hard way."

Hiking expert Chuck Fitzgerald has sound advice for pitchers in the visiting bullpen at Coors Field.

"First of all, if you must go into the forest, go with a friend if possible. Also, let people know where you are going and bring a cell phone and flares. This could have helped Clippard. Bring plenty of water, a blanket and some food rations. A compass would also be helpful," said Fitzgerald. "It is very easy to become disoriented past the center field fence at Coors Field. While it is beautiful, it can be dangerous. There have also been reports of mountain lions and grizzly bears roaming out there. Thank God nothing happened—this time."

"I survived on stale hot dog buns and nachos that were discarded into the forest by litterbugs from the bleachers," said Clippard. "It was a harrowing experience and I've learned my lesson."

After being examined by team trainers, Clippard was

deemed healthy and fit with no lingering side effects.

Nationals Manager Jim Riggleman said, "Clippard was missing for two days? Really? Is he ok? He is? Damn. The way he's pitching, it's too bad he couldn't stay lost for the rest of the season."

WHEN SPORTS WRITERS WRITE NEWS STORIES

Ronald Regan Dies
By Chip Goslin
Denver Post (6-5-2004)

Former sports movie icon and one-time Cubs broadcaster Ronald Reagan passed away yesterday, at the age of 93, in Los Angeles, California.

Reagan is probably best known for his portrayal of George Gipp, the star-crossed Notre Dame football player in the classic movie, *"Knute Rockne, All American."* He also starred as Hall of Fame pitcher, Grover Cleveland Alexander in *"The Winning Team."*

Reagan's athletic career began at Dixon High School in Illinois where he was a standout on the football team.

While enrolled at Eureka College in Illinois, he gained interest in acting and played football as well as many intramural sports.

Following college, Mr. Reagan took a job at a radio station in Iowa where he called Iowa Hawkeyes football. Later, he announced Chicago Cubs baseball, where he re-created the games in a Des Moines studio after getting details from the teletype machine.

In addition to sports, Reagan dabbled in politics in California and eventually became President of the United States for eight years.

He is survived by his wife Nancy and a bunch of kids and grandchildren.

THE POINTSPREAD

Iowa Head Coach Kirk Ferentz, despite beginning the season 5-0, was feeling the heat from disgruntled alumni.

Walter Scroggins, Class of '79 and a major booster of the Hawkeyes program, was upset with Ferentz. "Yeah, we're 5-0. Big deal. We're 1-4 against the spread and my bookie is cashing in. I'm not happy with Ferentz. Sportsmanship my ass!"

Another booster, Steve Lomano, asked, "Why can't Ferentz run up the score like Urban Meyer or Pete Carroll? He's costing a lot of people a lot of money but he doesn't seem to care. I can't bet against Iowa, so I'm in a serious quandary here."

Even the players are upset with their head coach. Starting quarterback Ricky Stanzi is really disturbed at the direction of the team under Ferentz.

Baffled by the anger of the fans Stanzi stated, "I'm out there busting my tail, trying to accumulate stats to impress the Heisman voters and the NFL scouts and Ferentz calls off the dogs. For example, a couple of weeks ago we're kicking the crap out of Florida International, 37-7 in the fourth quarter. Instead of letting me throw for another touchdown pass, we hand the ball off and run out the clock. Guess what? I'm pissed, and the fans are pissed. You got it, we were favored by thirty-two."

"I don't know why they are so upset with me," Coach Ferentz said. "We're off to a great start but the school president had me in her office and said we better start covering the spread or else. I guess I'll just do what I have to do to make everyone happy."

One Week Later ...

Despite trailing 24-20 with eleven seconds left in the game, and driving for the apparent winning touchdown, Iowa Head Coach Kirk Ferentz elected to kick a twenty-two yard field goal. The result was a dramatic 24-23 win for Illinois.

"Well, the mandate was that I better start beating the spread," said Ferentz. "Those were my specific orders from President Mason. I'm just following orders."

Prominent booster Walter Scroggins was irate with Ferentz's strategy. "Yeah, he covered and I won my bet, but we also lost the game. Why can't we win and cover. Just once. That's all I'm asking. Just one freaking time, win and cover. What's so hard about that?"

Iowa President Sally Mason confirmed the meeting in which she told the veteran coach that he needed to cover the spread at all costs. "Yes, I told Coach that, but I guess I also should have told him to win the game too. Hey, I'm really not that into football, but I'll learn. We play Ohio State next week. Are they any good?"

CHECK ME OUT DUDE!

Josh Rutland was "The Man" in the neighborhood. The 26-year-old thrilled his teenaged friends with his acrobatic bicycling skills.

Rutland could perform amazing stunts on his bike, and despite warnings from his parents, and other people sticking their noses in his business, nothing could stop the flamboyant bicycle showman.

"Man, I've just about done it all," recalled Rutland. "I once rode my bike on the ledge of a six story building, dude. I rode my bike on the interstate, dodging sick traffic. That was mad crazy, dude. I remember going down the stairs at the library and flying off a ramp and landing on the bed of a moving pickup truck. Check it out on YouTube, dude. It's radical."

However, the neighborhood was geeked over Rutland's next planned stunt, which he planned to finish with a massive splashdown in the family swimming pool.

The big day arrived and so did the crowd. Josh's best friend, Skeeter, was manning the video camera. It was time for the most bodacious stunt ever!

Josh began his decent down Williams Street. He picked up speed as he approached the ramp in his driveway. He hit the ramp perfectly and flew onto the roof of the two-story dwelling. He continued towards the back of the house and flew off the roof and hit the trampoline squarely with both wheels. He was then launched towards the pool. The bike landed perfectly in the water. Josh, though, was flung into the unyielding branch of the backyard oak tree. He landed hard and was hurt badly.

As Josh rolled around on the grass in severe pain, he raised his arms in triumph. While the stunt didn't go exactly as planned, he was stoked.

"I did it. I pulled it off," Josh grunted. "Skeeter, get that on YouTube now! This is awesome! Ugh, I think I broke my back."

It was then that Josh Rutland really felt the pain— pain he had never felt before. The pain came when Skeeter confessed, Uh, Josh, um, I forgot to turn the video camera on. My bad dude."

SHOOTING THE BREEZE

As they did every morning before work, three hard working, middle-age friends met at The Raceway Diner in Yonkers, New York, to have coffee and talk sports.

Carl, a maintenance man for the city's parks department, was thrilled that the Yankees signed lefthander CC Sabathia to a whopping seven year deal worth 161-million dollars. "He deserves every penny. The guy will lead us back to the World Series."

Jerry, who worked at the paper plant took a sip of his coffee and chimed in, "Don't forget Carl, we also got Burnett for 82-million. What a steal he is. I'm pumped up for that. Then add Teixeira to the mix for just 180-million. We're looking good. I just hope they keep spending on good players."

"Ha, the Mets ain't done nothing 'cept sign Frankie Rodriguez," chimed in Mike, a local delivery driver. "The Mets are cheapskates. That's why we're winners and the Mets are losers. Their payroll is only like 140-million. What a joke."

David Brody, a salesman from Birmingham, eavesdropped on the conversation from the booth next to the three friends. "Hey fellas, I overheard you guys talking baseball. Seems like you're big Yankee fans. Did you know that Alex Rodriguez will make more in two weeks than you guys will make in the next ten years combined?"

Silence ensued. The three friends then looked at each other then shrugged.

"Yeah, so?" Carl said.

SACRIFICES

The young children of Rosalind and Bernie Godfrey—Lisa, Amy, and Todd, were so excited for Christmas they could barely sleep. They were up at the crack of dawn.

The previous Christmas, the Godfrey kids made out like bandits—a haul for the ages. They expected another bountiful Christmas day.

The delighted siblings woke their parents up at 5:30 a.m., then ran down the stairs to the living room and towards the Christmas tree. They halted in their tracks. The Godfrey children stared at the absence of any presents under the brightly lit Christmas tree.

Crushed. Disappointed. Upset. Sad. Angry. All those emotions came into play as Bernie tried to soothe his forlorn and misty-eyed children.

"Kids, you know times are tough. We warned you not to get your hopes up. We did get you some small things and put them in your stockings, but the stuff on your lists, sorry. We had to make some sacrifices." Bernie smiled down at his children. "Remember, it is better to give than to receive. There are some kids who don't have enough to eat or a home to live in. You should count your blessings and say your prayers. Maybe next year will be better."

The kids were devastated, but understood. They knew they were blessed and felt bad for being so selfish.

Lisa, the oldest Godfrey kid, said to her subdued siblings, "You know, dad is right. We can't be greedy. We should be happy with what we have and remember those kids who are less fortunate."

The children then went into the kitchen to help mom

bake cookies. It was the best Christmas ever after all.

Meanwhile, Bernie snuck off to call his best friend and co-worker Vince.

"Vince, Merry Christmas!" Bernie said to his buddy. "Hey, I put in my down payment on the Yankees season tickets and re-upped my tickets for the Giants. I hate those premium fees. So, you still flying out with me for the Minnesota game Sunday?"

IT'S A MYSTERY

Former Giants Wide Receiver Plaxico Burress cannot understand where the commercial endorsements have gone.

"When I first came to New York from Pittsburgh I got endorsements from all sorts of companies," Burress commented. "It was a nice way to supplement my income. But now, the endorsements have dried up. It must be the economy."

Burress's agent, Drew Rosenhaus, is also mystified as to why his client is no longer reaping the endorsement rewards. "Plax is a great pitchman. Who wouldn't want the guy who caught the winning touchdown pass in the Super Bowl endorsing their product?" Rosenhaus looked into the camera. "I can't figure it out. I have no idea. Maybe it's because he's black."

Long-time public relations consultant Dawn Behnke countered with, "It may be Plaxico isn't getting endorsements because of the economy. Unfortunately, it could possibly be because he's an African-American."

Dawn looked out the window and sighed. "It also could be because he's a high-maintenance dumbass who shot himself in the leg at a nightclub and is in prison on weapons charges and may never play football again. Yeah, that could be it."

TRIVIA CHALLENGE

It was trivia night at *Calhoun's* in downtown Denver. The sports bar and grill was packed, as usual, and on this Friday night the trivia competition would be fierce.

The grand prize was an all-expense paid trip to San Diego to see the Broncos take on the Chargers. The tickets were right on the fifty yard line.

Jeremy Wendell was pumped up. Long known as "The Sports Trivia Geek" at work, Jeremy was confident he would win the trivia contest, again. He had won it eleven times in the previous year.

The rules stated a patron could only win once a month, otherwise the sports maven would win every week. But the prize was never as good as the one this night.

Jeremy spent the two weeks prior to the competition brushing up on his sports trivia. He watched ESPN Classic constantly. He poured over sports almanacs and media guides. He read old copies of The Sporting News and Sports Illustrated. Jeremy was prepared, confident and ready to kick some sports trivia ass! Get out the sun tan lotion, Jeremy Wendell was on his way to San Diego baby!

As the competition moved along, Jeremy was dominating as expected. His competitors were dropping like flies. There were two people left, Jeremy and some guy named Jones.

Jones correctly answered, "Ron Guidry," to the question: "Who was the American League Cy Young Award Winner in 1978?"

It was up to Jeremy to keep the competition alive with a correct answer.

The category was hockey. "Easy," said Jeremy to his

girlfriend Amanda. Or was it Cathy this week?

Anyway, Jeremy knew hockey like Pavarotti knows singing. Or, knew singing. He's dead now. Regardless, this trivia competition would go another round once Jeremy gave the answer. The contest was already four hours old and showed no signs of ending soon.

The trivia host gave the question. "Which team was coached by the all-time leading scorer in NHL history?"

Jeremy's first thought was, "Oh crap." He forgot that Wayne Gretzky was a head coach. What team did The Great One coach?

The crowd was silent. Tension was high. Jeremy had to guess.

"Um, the Edmonton Oilers?"

It was wrong and the drunk guy Jones won the trip to San Diego.

The correct answer was the Phoenix Coyotes.

"The Phoenix Coyotes! Holy %%$#, I forgot they even existed! Who knew?" Jeremy cried. "That was a trick question. I was duped!"

GOVERNMENT FUNDS CRUCIAL STUDY

Princeton researcher Dr. Willard Brandenberg is baffled as to why an athlete getting hit, kicked or punched in the groin brings uproarious laughter from everybody, except the guy getting hit in the nuts.

"In my study, it was easy to see why women laughed at men who got hit in the groin. Generally it's because women like to see a man in excruciating pain," Dr. Brandenberg said. "However, why men also laugh is beyond my comprehension."

The study found that people, men and women, have empathy when an athlete breaks a leg or gets a concussion, but when a male athlete gets drilled in the groin, hilarity often ensues.

Assistant researcher Michelle Morgan, when asked why she found it funny when a guy takes a shot to the balls, said, "Because it's just funny. Why? I don't know. It just is!"

The eight-hundred and fifty-thousand dollar study proved one thing to Dr. Brandenberg—the government will hand out grants for anything!

The joyous doctor raised his hands in triumph. "My next study will deal with why some people are fans of the Detroit Lions. I should get a grant of more than a million bucks on that one! I love America !"

JAYHAWK SKI TEAM FALTERS

For the 55th time in their fifty-five year history, the Kansas University downhill ski team finished last at the NCAA championships held in Park City, Utah.

"I just don't know what the problem is," said Kansas head coach Lars Stenson. "I mean, we do so well in training back home in Lawrence, but when we get out here to the downhill championships, we just mess the bed."

Mike Jessop, a junior for the Jayhawks said, "I knew Kansas was building a program, but I didn't know we were this bad historically. Otherwise, I would have gone to Colorado or Alaska to ski. How can we be so bad?"

Stenson, now in his fifth year guiding the Kansas downhill ski team said, "I've studied the situation and I can't figure it out. We've had good recruiting. We have top notch equipment. We have a supportive administration. I would even say we have a great coaching staff. But, for whatever reason, we finish last every year at the NCAA downhill skiing championships." He shrugged. "At least Nebraska is crappy in downhill skiing too."

SOUTH ATLANTIC FANTASY BASEBALL LEAGUE

Kirk Redwood from Salisbury, Maryland, studied all the statistics and scouting reports from the previous season of the New York-Penn, Northwest, Pioneer and Appalachian Leagues. Players from those rookie leagues would be filtering into the South Atlantic League this season and Redwood wanted to be prepared.

On the day of the South Atlantic League Fantasy Baseball Draft, Redwood was the first to arrive at the Waffle House. He took his place in the private party room in the back. He brought several volumes of scouting reports. Every player who might enter or return to the South Atlantic League this season, had been charted and scouted in extreme detail.

He prepared by reading books on fantasy baseball strategy. His draft board was complete, the result of many hours burning the midnight oil. Redwood was eager, ready and confident to assemble a championship fantasy team.

The draft was to begin at 9 a.m. sharp. "Must be a late arriving crowd," thought Redwood as he was the only team owner in the room at 9:15. At noon, Redwood began to worry.

"Gamesmanship," Redwood surmised.

Two days, one-hundred thirty waffles, fifty-five donuts and sixty-three cups of coffee later, Kirk Redwood left the Waffle House. He was dismayed and upset.

The seven other would-be owners of the South Atlantic Fantasy Baseball League, decided to eschew the upstart fantasy league and join an established Major League

Baseball fantasy league. Nobody alerted Kirk.

The despondent Redwood walked along Old Ocean City road and tossed his books and scouting reports in a dumpster. There would be no fantasy baseball glory this season for Kirk.

THE DISTRACTION

Bryan Wright worked as a manager at an investment firm. His work week usually stretched into sixty or seventy long, hard hours. When his work week ended, all he wanted was just one thing—to simply enjoy a weekend of football, undisturbed.

Jake Houser also worked for the same firm and was under the direction of Wright. Houser worked long, hard hours as well and wanted just one thing when the weekend arrived—Mrs. Wright.

Alison Wright, who had met Jake at a company picnic that summer, took an immediate liking to the younger financial whiz. The feeling was mutual.

The attractive Alison complained to Jake, "When football season starts he won't even know I exist. I could be gone all day and the only thing he would miss would be me making him ham and turkey sandwiches."

The pair hatched a well-thought out plan.

On the first weekend of the NFL season, Alison and Jake secretly met in a nearby town and had lunch at the Del Piano Restaurant. Then they settled in for an afternoon of fun behind closed doors.

Meanwhile, Bryan stayed at home and watched a multitude of football games without any distraction or interruption.

At work on Monday, Jake was a nervous wreck. He didn't feel too guilty, but he was paranoid. Bryan greeted him warmly and that eased Jake's tension.

"He has no idea," thought Jake. "This will be easier than I thought."

The weeks went by. Alison and Jake had their fun on

the weekends while Bryan watched football.

Just as the playoffs rolled around, Alison told Bryan that she had to stay home the following Sunday to work on a few projects.

This situation warranted a phone call.

"Hey Jake, Bryan here. How are you?" asked Wright.

"I'm doing fine sir," said Jake. "Everything ok?"

"Sure, yeah, everything is fine. Hey, I wanted to ask you a question. Have you ever been to the Del Piano Restaurant?"

Jake's stomach jumped into his throat. He paused and said, "Um, well, no. Is it good?"

"Look Jake, I need you to take Alison to Del Piano's again on Sunday. I'll foot the bill. I just can't have her here, especially during the playoffs!"

"I don't know what you mean Bryan."

"Tell the maitre d', Angelo, that I said hello. And Jake, thanks for freeing up my Sundays. Hey, man, gotta run. See you at the office on Monday."

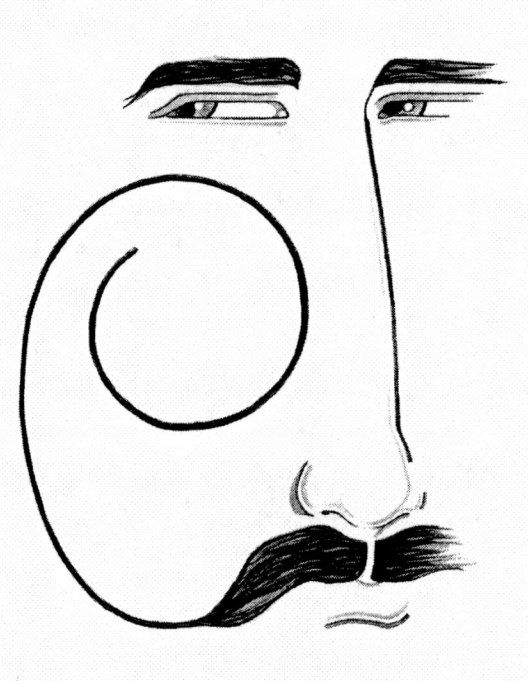

FINGERS FACES REALITY

The man stared into the mirror. He looked closely and didn't like what he saw.

It was at that moment that baseball Hall of Famer, Rollie Fingers realized that his trademark handlebar mustache looked stupid and he had wasted untold hours of his life twirling and waxing it.

"What was I thinking way back when?" Fingers said to former teammate Reggie Jackson. "I mean, why couldn't I have been satisfied with a regular mustache instead of a high-maintenance handlebar stash? Ugh."

"I never had the heart to tell Rollie that his handlebar mustache looked silly," Mrs. Fingers said.

"He liked it so I figured, hey, there are worse things he could be doing than twirling and curling his mustache ten hours a day."

When asked if he was going to finally shave his mustache off, the pitching great said, "I already tried, but the thing has fossilized onto my face. I can't get rid of it. Now I'm destined to live the rest of my life with this stupid looking handlebar mustache."

THAT SINKING FEELING

Hoping to gain a competitive edge, Steve Treskopf figured the use of ankle weights would be beneficial in his quest to become the best high school swimmer in the county.

"Ankle weights will make my workouts tougher," Treskopf told his friends. "I'll be stronger and faster and I'll be able to land a scholarship."

After receiving the water-proof ankle weights in the mail, Treskopf was eager to try them out.

Shortly after diving into the pool during practice, Steve Treskopf sunk to the bottom and drowned.

Police detective Richie Murphy said an investigation is continuing, but the weights on his ankles could have been a contributing factor in his untimely demise.

SCALPED

Jason Murray hated ticket scalpers, and with good reason.

Sure there are some honorable scalpers. Ok, there are no honorable scalpers.

Jason was usually able to get a ticket to a sold out game with a little haggling and patience. But he got burned more than a few times and Murray had trouble letting it go.

He once paid $75 for a ticket that he was told was on the fifty yard line. Instead, he found himself in the last row of the upper deck near the end zone at old Three Rivers Stadium.

On another occasion, Murray paid $100 for a seat at Wrigley Field on the first base line. "Perfect view," he was told. Yes, it was a perfect view, of a steel beam.

Same thing happened to him at venerable Boston Garden. "Great seat," he was told. He ended up behind a cement column and could only see half the ice.

The episode that really ticked off Murray though was Super Bowl XL at Detroit's Ford Field between the Seahawks and Steelers.

"I wanted to see the game badly, so I decided to dip into my savings and attend my first Super Bowl," recalled Murray. "I bought a ticket from a scalper. Cost me 700 bucks. When I went to the Stadium, my ticket was scanned. The next thing I know I'm getting arrested for having a counterfeit ticket. No, I didn't get to see the game. Thankfully the judge threw out the case the next day. But I spent Super Bowl Sunday in a smelly jail cell
in Detroit. I was pissed. Figuratively and literally."

Murray had enough. It was payback time and he had

an idea.

Game three of the 2007 World Series at Coors Field in Denver was, of course, sold out. Murray traveled to Denver with the goal of getting into the Red Sox-Rockies game for free.

While wandering around the neighborhood surrounding Coors Field, Murray encountered many scalpers. Tickets were going for more than 300 dollars.

About fifteen minutes before game time, Murray engaged a scalper in dialogue.

"How much?" Murray asked a shady looking guy holding a ticket.

"400 dollars," was the response.

"How do I know it's real and not a fake?" asked Murray.

"Of course it's real," replied the annoyed scalper.

"I've been burned before. How about I take the ticket to the ticket-taker and let him tell me? If it's legit, I'll come right back and give you 400 bucks," Murray said.

The scalper thought for a moment, then agreed.

Murray walked across Blake Street and approached a ticket-taker. He showed him his ticket and asked, "Is this a legit ticket?"

The worker looked at it closely and said, "Yes."

Murray handed the ticket to the man, pushed through the turnstile, then turned and waved to the scalper who wasn't very happy when he realized what had happened. Murray disappeared into the stadium, blending in with the crowd.

Being a sharp guy, Murray didn't even sit in his seat behind home plate, preferring to stand on the left field concourse during the game. He wanted to make sure the scalper didn't get into the game and find him sitting in the seat that matched the ticket he scammed.

Murray felt good. He felt vindicated. He ripped off a scalper and it felt great!

He was disappointed the Rockies lost, but it was a fun night anyway and he would have a great story to tell—initially with his jaw wired shut.

As Jason Murray left Coors Field that chilly October evening, there was somebody waiting for him.

Scalper Antoine Robinson spotted Murray, followed him down a side street, tapped Murray on the shoulder and said, "Remember me?"

Good night Jason.

THE ENFORCER LEAVES TURF FOR LIONS

Senior Artificial Turf radio producer Don Apodaca has left the long-time sports program and taken a job as President and General Manager of the Detroit Lions.

"I hate to leave the show," said Apodaca, "but I needed a new challenge. I'm the man to rebuild the Detroit Lions."

Lions owner William Clay Ford said, "My grandson was listening to some sports radio program on, what do you call it …oh, the internet, whatever that is. I heard this guy, Apodaca, sharing some strong opinions on football. I was intrigued. When I heard his nickname was 'The Enforcer' I was sold. We need toughness and Don 'The Enforcer' Apodaca is our guy. And hey, he can't do worse than Matt Millen."

Many NFL insiders were totally caught off guard and perplexed with Ford's move.

ESPN's Freddie Coleman said, "I respect Don's football knowledge, but to run an NFL franchise? I'm not sure about this one. Ok, I'll be candid. It's the worst move in the history of professional sports, but that's the Lions for ya."

Further infuriating the dozens of existing Lions fans, Ford gave Apodaca a fifteen year contract.

"I presented Mr. Ford with my fifteen year plan to win Super Bowl 58," said Apodaca. "If I gave him a three or four year plan, that doesn't bode well for my job security. I told Mr. Ford: You've waited fifty-two years for a championship, what's another fifteen?"

EXTREME FISHING SHOW TOO EXTREME

First there was *Extreme Bass Fishing*, a television program that closely resembled non-extreme bass fishing.

Competitive Fishing Commissioner Dave Porter said, "There really wasn't anything that extreme about *Extreme Bass Fishing* on TV. That's when we made a tragic mistake."

The mistake was inventing *Extreme Piranha Fishing*.

Part of the excitement and fun of *Extreme Bass Fishing* was watching one of the participants standing in a boat and try to reel in a bass, but then lose his balance and fall overboard. The highlight shows were filled with such hilarity.

But during the recent *Extreme Piranha Fishing* show, aired on ESPN from Tampa, Florida, Johnny Garcia fell out of his boat while struggling with a feisty piranha.

"I told Commissioner Porter that stocking the lake with piranhas might not be a good idea," claimed Ray Torvais. "He said, 'Ratings Ray, think ratings!' Well, my best friend is gone. Completely. In twelve seconds. It was horrible. But at least I'll get his fishing equipment and boat, unless his greedy wife gets involved. She's why Johnny took up fishing in the first place, to get away from that selfish bitch!"

NOT QUITE READY

During a recent training session at the 20th Street Gym in Denver, Colorado, veteran boxing trainer Hipolito Maldonado declared welterweight Billy Gensch not quite ready to begin his professional boxing career.

"The kid was really working over the speedbag," said Maldonado. "He's got nice hands, but he put his mug too close to the bag and it knocked him out cold. Amazing."

"Yeah, the bag caught me good. I got careless and got tagged," Gensch said. "But it's not like it has never happened before."

"In the history of boxing, ain't no one been knocked out by a speedbag. Not one." Maldonado went on, "Look, I can teach the kid footwork. I can teach the kid how to throw combinations. I can teach defense, but I can't overcome a glass jaw."

"If Hip won't train me I'll just get another trainer," said the southpaw. "With the right trainer I have no doubt I'll become a world champeen."

With that, Gensch walked out of the 20th Street Gym for the final time. The wind caught a hot dog wrapper and it hit Gensch squarely in the face, thereby knocking him out and putting his boxing career on hold.

COACH'S SON
"INSPIRATIONAL"

Josh Einart, from Port Charlotte, Florida is an inspiration. The 11-year-old is enthusiastic, exuberant, mischievous and charming. In other words, a normal young boy, except for one thing. Actually two things—Josh was born without arms.

But Josh refuses to let his lack of arms slow him down. He doesn't want sympathy or pity. He is an inspiration to everyone he meets and nowhere can that be found more than on the baseball field.

Josh's dad and little league coach for the Port Charlotte Rangers, Spencer, knew that Josh could not only play, but inspire his teammates.

"Look," Spencer defended, "even if Josh wasn't my son I'd still put him at shortstop and bat him third. He's our best player. I mean if Jim Abbott can make it to the big leagues without a hand, then why can't Josh make it without arms?"

But the Rangers are off to a tough 0-8 start.

"Our team sucks," said pitcher Danny Paulson, "but because Josh is the coach's son he has to play shortstop and bat third."

Left fielder Eric Salerno added, "Yeah, why can't he be the bat boy or something? I mean, I'm sorry he has no arms but he's hurting the team."

One parent even commented, "That freak at shortstop is giving handicapped athletes everywhere a bad name."

Spencer Einart has heard the whispers and chooses

to ignore them.

"It hurts," said Spencer. "But when I put Josh on the All-Star team, then what can they say?"

Josh has a unique style to compensate for his lack of arms. He hits by resting his bat on his left shoulder and holding it in place with his jaw. He then turns his body and makes contact, or tries to, with the bat coming through the strike zone.

"Sort-of like people holding a phone when they have their hands full," said Josh. "I'm pretty good at it, but have some trouble trying to check my swing."

He fields the baseball, by using the proper technique of getting in front of the ball, with a glove attached to his left knee.

One question people are asking is, how does Josh throw the ball?

"Well, let me field a ball first," said Josh. "Then I'll figure out the throwing part. I'm guessing I might have to kick it over to first base."

Like his young teammates, Josh is learning the game as he goes along. With the coaching he's getting from his dad, he expects to improve and remain an inspiration to handicapable athletes everywhere.

"I do like being an inspiration," Josh said. "It's great, but it gets a little awkward when people ask for my autograph."

CHEER CHEER FOR OLD NOTRE DAME

He woke up ready for battle, glad that it was a day game instead of a night game. There would be less time to kill and less time for the nerves to take hold.

His Fighting Irish of Notre Dame were anticipating mauling their rivals from the West. The sooner he got to Notre Dame Stadium and put on his uniform, the better. He knew the Trojans of Southern Cal were in big trouble.

He got to the stadium and noted the big crowds gathered outside the football cathedral. This wasn't just any game. It was a huge game with National Championship implications. The slightest mistake could be very, very costly.

He saw USC Coach Pete Carroll walking towards the locker room with a big smile on his face. He wondered how the coach could be so relaxed. He couldn't wait until his Irish wiped that smile off his mug.

Game time approached. Soon it would be time to take the field. Time to put on the uniform. He checked his equipment. He sat by himself in silence, to put himself in the proper frame of mind to defeat the Trojans.

This is what he worked for all season long. This is why he put in the extra practice time. This is why he worked himself to exhaustion at summer camp.

The excitement was palpable. It was time to hit the Notre Dame Stadium turf. Larry Pfeiffer adjusted the chinstrap on his hat, put on his white gloves, gently picked up his clarinet and eagerly joined his band mates.

The vaunted Southern Cal marching band would be no match today for his band, The University of Notre Dame's Marching Band—The Band of the Fighting Irish!

PROMISE DELIVERED

Dave Gesner of Yonkers was fired up. The garage sale netted him a cool $450. The sale of the junky car he fixed up brought another $1,400. Helping paint his brother-in-law's house and build a deck the past four weekends added $600 more. He closed out an old savings account for just $225, but every little bit helped.

The canoe he used twice, brought $500 from the classified ad he posted. The next piece of the puzzle was re-financing the house. For that he was able to free up a tidy $7,300 and the personal loan from the bank brought in $2,000 more.

Now, all Dave needed to do was work some overtime at the job for the next month and he would raise an extra thousand dollars or so. That would put him at around $14,000.

Dave was excited that he could finally fulfill a promise he made to his wife and two kids.

"Hey honey," Dave shouted to Brenda. "I did it! We'll be able to attend a game at the new Yankee Stadium this season!"

BAD BOXING NICKNAMES

Every boxer has a nickname. Some are better than others. The Artificial Turf radio program has polled its listeners, historians, journalists and former pugilists to come up with the worst nicknames in boxing history.

Here is the list of the top sixteen bad boxing nicknames:

16) "Bleeding" Bob Adams
15) Charlie "The Chump" O'Reilly
14) "Toothless" Tommy Traber
13) Stan "Standing 8 count" Smolinski
12) "Senseless" Stevie Myers
11) Denard "Beaten Down" Brown
10) Billy "Brain Contusion" Reyes
9) Frankie "Fist Face" Gonzales
8) "No Chance" Chase Burns
7) Dougie "Double Vision" Delaney
6) "Facial Fracture" Freddie Furman
5) "Timid" Timm McLaughlin
4) Danny "Detached Retina" Reynolds
3) "Luckless" Larry Lazar
2) Davey "Ruptured Spleen" Green
1) "Where Am I?" Walter Washington

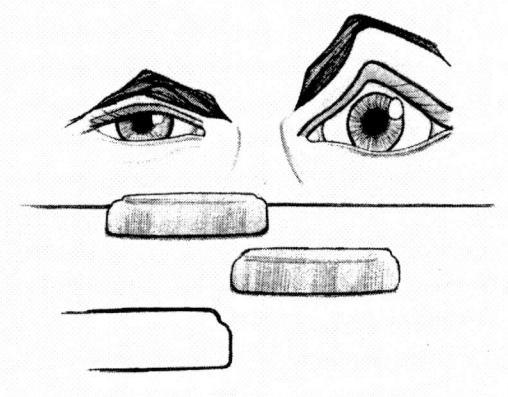

CHECKERS CHAMP PEEVED

Kyle Turner was patient long enough. The World Checkers Champion had reached his boiling point.

"Where are the endorsements? Where are the appearances on Letterman? Where are the easy women? What is going on here?" ranted the 39-year-old Turner.

From the age of six, when he first fell in love with the sport of checkers, Turner devoted his life to becoming the best in the world.

"My dad told me, 'Son, when you become checkers champ, you'll have it made.' Unfortunately Pop didn't live long enough to see me accomplish my dream. He knew I would become the champ, but he was wrong about the riches part," said Turner.

The undisputed checkers champ aimed most of his wrath at World Chess Champion, Viswanathan Anand from India.

"I see this guy on TV and he's riding in his private jet or hanging out at the pool with a bunch of super models," rued Turner. "No one can even pronounce his name, but he's living the life just because he's the chess champ? What am I, sliced brisket?"

Despite the lack of recognition and respect, Turner moves on. He is undaunted in his quest to be the greatest checkers player ever.

"I want to be known as the best of all-time," Turner said. "I want to be even more well known than ...than ...well, that guy who currently is known as the greatest checkers champ ever!"

Turner is set to defend his title next month against fourth grade challenger David Cornell at the World

Checkers Championship to be held in the basement of Valley View Elementary School in Pompton Plains, New Jersey.

RAMIFICATIONS

Pablo Salvador was seconds away from his lifelong dream. Roy Franklin was wobbly and his hold on the title was tenuous.

Salvador delivered a devastating blow, a right cross to the jaw of Franklin, then followed with a crushing left hook. It was lights out for Franklin.

The referee counted Franklin out and there was a new WBC World Welterweight Champeen.

It was a chaotic scene, at the MGM Grand in Las Vegas, as Salvador's triumphant handlers entered the ring, as did a bunch of security guards, officials and media members, including HBO boxing commentator Larry Merchant.

"Congratulations Pablo," began Merchant. "When did you feel you had Franklin in trouble?"

"Thank you Larry," said a jubilant Salvador. "First and foremost I would like to thank my Lord and savior Jesus Christ. Without him I wouldn't be here today. Praise be to Jesus. I'd also like to thank my wife Esmerelda and my kids Pablo Junior, Raymondo and Maria."

Esmerelda, a deeply religious woman who despised boxing, was fuming as she looked at the TV screen. She thought, "Are you kidding me Pablo? You haven't seen the inside of a church in years! How can you take the Lord's name in vain?"

Meanwhile, at her Long Beach home, Pablo's girlfriend, a suddenly furious Gloria Hernandez watched as she shouted at the TV, "What? Wife? Kids? Oh no he di'ent!"

It was the greatest night of Pablo Salvador's

professional career, but little did he know that his life was about to get slightly more complicated.

DEAD AIM DUKE

In a showdown of two of the all-time PBA greats, Norm Duke took control of the match against Walter Ray Williams in the fourth frame.

By the seventh frame it was basically over. Williams couldn't convert a couple of 7-10 splits and Duke had tossed seven straight strikes. With the prestigious Columbus Invitational in the bag, the only question now was if Duke could finish with a flourish and a perfect 300 game.

Throughout the tournament the popular Duke charmed the crowd with his affable personality and dazzling bowling skills. Everyone at the AMF Bowling Center pulled for Duke. All except one exceptionally loud and irritating heckler.

The scruffy, obnoxious, overweight boor, decked out in Ohio State gear, was all over Duke throughout the four day tournament.

The refined Duke ignored the agitator, which further garnered him good will amongst the Columbus crowd.

As Duke hit his ninth strike in a row, the classy Walter Ray Williams applauded. He too was pulling for Duke to roll a perfecto.

Another strike for Duke. That was 10 in a row. He needed just two more. The intensity and drama, that is bowling at its finest, was building with each passing moment.

Although Williams finished with a respectable 233, all eyes were on Duke. The tension was unbearable as Duke rolled his 11th straight strike.

Across the country, people watching on television called their family and friends urging them to turn on their sets.

Duke was ready to roll his 12th strike. Who would bet against the focused Duke? After all, pressure was a foreign word to Duke. He was steady and unflappable. He had rolled more than 50 perfect games in his spectacular Hall of Fame career. But this one, if he could pull it off, against Walter Ray Williams, would be extra special. Even the heckler had been subdued the last few frames.

Duke put his hand over the ball return dryer, his powerful right arm dangling at his side. He grabbed his colorful ball and stared down the lane. The crowd was completely silent. You could see Duke's incredible athleticism as he began his approach. His head was steady. He drew his right arm back. For bowling aficionados, Duke's grace and power was a thing of beauty.

Just a fraction of a second before Duke released, what was likely to be his 12th consecutive strike, Craig Dumont, the idiot heckler, yelled as loud as he could, "DON'T CHOKE DUKE!"

Startled, the ball came out of Duke's hand awkwardly. It drifted to the left, missed the head pin and resulted in just seven pins knocked down. There would be no perfect game today for Duke.

The crowd was horrified. They were ready to beat the living crap out of loudmouth Dumont who ruined a potential 300 game. But then Duke, ever the gentleman, raised his hand to quell the angry crowd. He looked at Dumont and gave him a slight smile. Dumont felt relieved.

Then Duke walked out of the bowling center to his RV in the parking lot. A moment later Duke strolled back into the building. He walked over to Dumont and, without fanfare, pulled a .45 pistol from his waistband and capped the man right, who cost him a 300 game, right between the eyes.

Duke demonstrated the same accurate precision that he used over and over again in his illustrious bowling career. When Dumont hit the floor, Duke plugged him three more times for good measure.

Following the shooting, Duke calmly walked over to the tournament sponsors, posed for pictures with the tourney directors and his oversized cardboard check, took his Columbus Invitational Championship trophy and exited the bowling center. He faced a long trip in his RV to the next tournament, the Reno Open.

Four months later, it took a jury only four minutes to acquit Duke of all charges.

No one ever heckled Norm Duke again.

AMERICAN IDLE SNUBBED

After carefully considering all the facts and stats, the Yankees organization has decided not to retire former pitcher Carl Pavano's number 45.

"That isn't to say we won't retire Carl's number in the future," said Yankees owner Hal Steinbrenner. "I'm sure we'll revisit this situation if Carl gets elected to the Hall of Fame."

Pavano, known as 'American Idle' during his stay in pinstripes, is now taking up space on the Twins' roster. He was perplexed over the apparent Yankee snub.

"I gave that team everything I had," said an upset Pavano. "I gave them nine wins over the four seasons I was there. Nine wins they might not have gotten if I wasn't there. How would you feel if you were in my shoes?"

When reminded that he made (stole) thirty-eight million dollars from the Yankees and spent more time on the disabled list than a dead man, the irritated Pavano said, "And what exactly is your point?"

WORST LOCKER ROOM
SPEECH EVER

This would be the first appearance in the state championship game for the Palisades High Porcupines since 1937.

The entire town and state was captivated by the story of the Porcupines rise from the ashes. Just a year ago, the historically dismal Porcupines finished 1-9 and there was talk of disbanding the program.

But somehow, some way, the Porcupines went 8-2 in the regular season, won three playoff games and were now moments away from taking on the mighty Marauders of Marchesani High, the four-time defending state champs.

The eager Porcupines finished their pre-game warm-ups and returned to the locker room. The excitement the players felt was like nothing they had experienced before. The semi-final win over Passaic High was thrilling, but this was the championship game. Tension and nervousness filled the room.

Head Coach Frank Sayers was a master motivator. He would certainly provide a calming effect and have his team peaking emotionally come kickoff time.

Sayers walked into the room. He surveyed the situation and decided a fire and brimstone speech was unnecessary.

"Gentlemen, we've exceeded all expectations this year. Don't put pressure on yourselves. Remember, we shouldn't be here. We really, really got lucky this year you have to admit." He continued. "I know you are thinking that there is no way you can beat Marchesani High today. And you know something? You're right. I don't want to get your hopes up, but that doesn't mean we can't go out there and give our best."

Sayers had his hand in his pockets and looked around the room. After a lengthy pause, he resumed his pre-game talk. "A lot of teams would rather lose in the championship game than not even be here. I bet all the high school kids who die in car crashes due to underage drunken driving would like to be here. Same with the kids who are born with birth defects or mental deficiencies. What about the kids who come from broken homes and end up on drugs or in a juvenile detention center? They would love the chance to lose in the championship game. You have the opportunity to go out there and lose. And you can lose in one of two ways—you can get blown out and lose by fifty or you can go out there and lose by just three touchdowns. It's your choice. Either way, I'm proud of you guys. Now let's go out there and try not to get hurt and to lose with dignity. After the game, I don't want anyone hanging their heads. Be sure to congratulate your opponents. Now let's go guys!"

The packed stadium watched the hard charging Marauders take the field, running through the paper banner held by the cheerleaders that displayed the school's ferocious logo. The Marauders were fired up, slapping each other upside the helmet and working themselves into a frenzy. Kickoff was moments away.

Next, the Porcupines took the field. They casually strolled to the sidelines. It looked like pre-game exuberance and energy had been replaced by fear and trepidation.

The final score: Marchesani High 63, Palisades High 0.

"I'm not surprised," said Coach Sayers. "We just weren't ready to play. Why? I have no idea."

THE STALKER

Ronald "Buddy" Komarsky has a huge crush on LPGA star Natalie Gulbis.

Every golf fan admires Gulbis. What is not to like? She's smart, beautiful and athletic. But Komarsky wishes to take his stalking to an elite level.

"I really would like to stalk Natalie, full-time," said Komarsky. "I think she would actually like me as her own personal stalker."

He smiled revealing his crooked, tobacco stained teeth.

"Even though people think I'm creepy, I would say to them that I'm not THAT creepy. I'm quite harmless actually," the portly 52-year-old Komarsky said. "I would just try to win Natalie's affection," the life-long bachelor revealed as he lamented his financial situation. "The problem is that it costs money to be an effective stalker, money I don't have. I mean, following her to all the tournaments, hanging out in her neighborhood, sending her expensive gifts. Ugh. (pause) I wish I knew how the professional stalkers do it."

Komarsky, a security guard and part-time Boy Scout Troop Leader, continued. "I'd be an excellent stalker, I really would. But I just don't have the time or money." Buddy stared into space, ran his hand through his dandruff-laced combover, then shrugged. "So, I guess I'll just have to keep on stalking that junior high cheerleader who lives down the street."

AN EARLY RETIREMENT

Kevin McShea's major league debut was even better than he dreamed. After toiling for eight long years in the minors, McShea finally made it to "The Show" when the Royals called him up in September from Omaha.

"A dream come true," said McShea.

But McShea became disillusioned as he sat the bench for three weeks before getting his chance to bat. On the next to last day of the season, against the Twins, McShea's dream awakened. The journeyman outfielder was called on to pinch-hit in the bottom of the seventh inning at Kauffman Stadium.

"I remember stepping up to the plate against Boof Bonser," recalled McShea. "Normally, I would have been nervous making my big league debut, but I thought how can I not get a hit off some guy named Boof?"

Sure enough, McShea connected on a 1-1 pitch and drilled it into the right field bullpen. In the ninth inning, McShea, patrolling left, caught the final out in the Royals 8-3 victory. It was the last game McShea ever played.

"I was sitting in the locker room and it dawned on me. I hit a home run in my only at-bat in the major leagues. I own a 1.000 batting average. Even catching one fly ball put my fielding percentage at 1.000. I figured, if I retire now I'll go down in history as the most perfect baseball player ever!"

So McShea quit the game. He didn't want to go back to the minors the following season. He didn't want to struggle to make it back to the majors. He wanted a baseball career, however short, that people would remember.

Three years later, McShea was working for $10 an

hour in a Portland lumberyard and wondered, "Maybe I did call it quits a little prematurely. But at least I'm happy. Wait a minute. Ok. I'll level with you. I'm the biggest idiot in the world to give up playing baseball to work in this crappy lumberyard. Big deal, a 1.000 batting average and a home run in my only at-bat."

McShea stared ahead and continued. "I gave up on my dreams, my future and I'm ridiculed behind my back everyday for my dumbass decision. I hate my life!"

RUN DEWEY RUN

Dewey Parker, 26, was captivated by the "Running of the Bulls" in Pamplona, Spain.

For years he wanted to participate and run with the bulls. Even with his G.E.D. and 57 IQ, Dewey knew it was dangerous. Perhaps a little too dangerous.

"Plus, I don't have the money to travel to Asia," said Dewey.

Instead, the El Paso, Texas resident decided to journey to the nearby Mexican town of Chihuahua for the annual "Running with the Chihuahuas."

His big day came and Dewey was excited. The gates of the course opened and Dewey and two-hundred other schmucks ran for their lives with hundreds of snappy, yappy Chihuahuas snipping at their heels.

Some runners were trampled. Others were eaten alive. Dewey was lucky. He escaped only with bruises and forty-something bite marks.

"Man, those little suckers are nasty," said Dewey. "I couldn't get them off me. They are like land sharks. I actually think running with the Bulls would be safer."

When told of his nephew's "Running with the Chihuahuas", Dewey's Uncle Pete said sadly, "Dewey's not well in the head."

RASHEED

You would think Rasheed Washington would be a great athlete. You can certainly imagine him taking off from the free throw line and slamming home a rim-rattling dunk. You could see him evading a linebacker with a slick cut and outracing the safeties sixty yards for a touchdown. You could also see him winning a one-hundred meter dash with ease.

So you could understand the excitement of the coaches at Apple Valley High School when they saw the name Rasheed Washington on the attendance sheet.

Rasheed, the new kid, was immediately summoned from his first class to meet with Athletic Director Lew Slattery.

"You're Rasheed Washington?" asked the confused Slattery.

"Yes." Rasheed replied.

"Really?"

"Yes sir."

"Hmmm. You sure about that?"

"Yes sir."

"Ok. Well then, never mind. So, um, welcome to Apple Valley. Well, uh, Rasheed, you better get back to class."

The new student shrugged his shoulders. Then, the only white kid on the planet named Rasheed, headed back to his tenth grade algebra class.

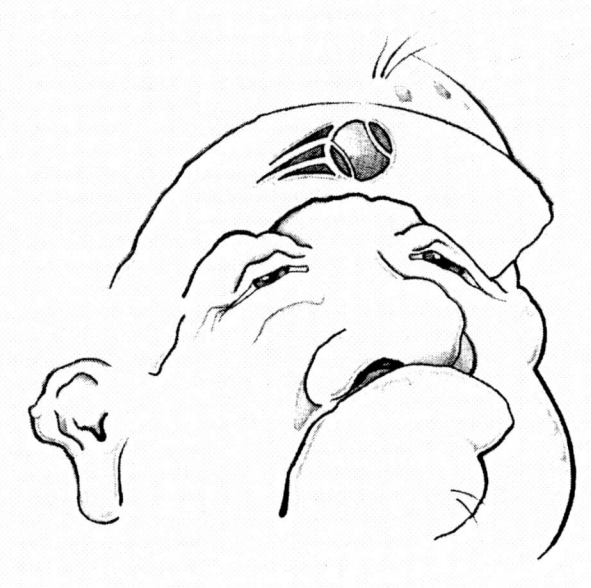

THE KLIPPSTEIN DYNASTY

For the third consecutive year, Artie Klippstein has won the Colorado State Tennis Championship in the 90 and over division at the Pinehurst Country Club in Denver.

The 93-year-old Klippstein boiled over with excitement.

"I'm happy and thrilled to be a three-time champ. This is especially gratifying since I never won anything in my life, until three years ago," Klippstein said. "And I just took up tennis four years ago!"

Artie lost in his first tournament appearance to 92-year-old Bernie Decker.

Unfortunately, Decker passed away shortly after. One factor for Klippstein's success could be that he is the only person, in his age group, who has entered the tournament the past three years.

MALE CHEERLEADERS ELIMINATED

After just one game, the San Francisco 49ers have scrapped their new male cheerleading squad.

"We thought we would appeal to the large homosexual population in our city by employing male cheerleaders in Speedos on the sidelines," said Michael Williams, vice president of marketing. "It seemed like a good idea at the time."

Debbie Carlson, team cheerleading director said, "I told Mike that male cheerleaders wouldn't work. And to put them in Speedos? Ugh, that was just a bad decision."

Tyler Laremieux, a 49ers season ticket holder and a homosexual, was also in favor of getting rid of the new male cheerleaders. "Look, even as a homo, I find men in Speedos disgusting and inappropriate, at least at a football game. Nobody should have to look at that."

Carlson added, "We'll keep our regular cheerleaders of course. We have brand new hot skimpy outfits that will accentuate the cleavage and curves of our girls. We also have incorporated some new really erotic sexy dance moves. It will be much more appropriate and family friendly for our fans than the male cheerleader experiment."

A DOG'S LIFE

Bailey was a Jack Russell Terrier and the two-time defending champ in "Best in Show" at the Westminster Dog Show, the World Series of dog competitions.

Owner Tiffany Morgan spoiled Bailey and paid little attention to her other dog Buddy, who quickly proved he was not "show dog" material.

The obedient Bailey, always primped and pampered, was envious though of Buddy.

"Buddy, although dumber than a doorknob, gets to live a fun life, the life of a dog," thought Bailey. "I have to behave all the time. I hate when these old guys feel me up when they judge me."

The other show dogs hated Bailey because she was a champion.

The finals at Madison Square Garden drew the usual huge crowd. Bailey was expected to defend her crown easily; however, the champion canine had other ideas.

During the final judging portion of the competition, Bailey was on the table getting looked over by the judges.

It's here where things became hazy for Bailey's owner Tiffany.

"I don't know what happened," said the stunned Morgan. "Things just got out of control."

Bailey intentionally drooled all over the table and while a judge was touching her hind quarters, Bailey urinated on his hand. She then bit him, jumped off the table, ran from her handlers and defecated on the arena floor. To avoid capture she ran out of sight of the bewildered crowd.

Needless to say that was the end of Bailey's show dog career. No more daily baths. No more gourmet dinners. No more pampering. It was Alpo and chasing Frisbees from here on out.

In the blink of an eye, Bailey became a real dog.

INSOMNIATIC DISCOVERY

A decade long study by Boca Raton Junior College researchers has discovered that tennis cures insomnia.

"We studied hundreds of insomniacs," said lead researcher Doctor Leland C. Vonderstein. "Nothing we tried to cure insomnia really worked."

Then one January evening during a late night broadcast of the Australian Open, Vonderstein noticed several insomniacs in the television room were out cold; sleeping like a group of hung over college kids in an early morning biology class.

The next night, the insomniacs were gathered again in the television room of the treatment center.

"They were watching infomercials and were wide awake. By the way, that *ShamWow* thing is awesome even if the pitchman is an annoying jagoff," recalled Vonderstein. "Anyway, I turned the channel to the tennis tournament, despite the protestations of the case study participants. Within minutes they were sound asleep. Out cold. One guy was literally out cold. He died, but I think the fact that he was ninety-six had more to do with it than tennis, but we'll study that too."

Vonderstein and his assistants put two and two together and realized that the somnolent sport of tennis cures insomnia.

"I thank Dr. Vonderstein from the bottom of my now sleepy heart," said John Stickler. "Now, all I have to do is pop in a tape of a tennis match and I'm a visitor to sleepyland. Unless it's a match of one of those hot female Russian players."

DISINGENUOUS

The door to the manager's office opened, then slammed shut.

"If I don't hit leadoff and play everyday, then I want out of here," threatened Dane Bramage to his manager. "I'm sick and tired of being platooned and my agent is already working the phones."

Veteran manager John Namovicz replied, "Dane, listen, I'm trying to do what is best for the ball club. And you're hitting .237."

"I don't care about the ball club," bellowed Bramage. "I'm hitting .237 because I'm not playing everyday. You couldn't manage a mall kiosk. This organization doesn't pay me eight-million a year to sit the bench or hit ninth. I want out!"

Following his tirade, the angry shortstop exited the manager's office and walked through the clubhouse to his locker. Several media members were waiting for him.

"Word is that you are unhappy batting down in the batting order," said veteran baseball scribe Petey Caldera.

"Where did you hear that?" replied a surprised Bramage. "I don't care where I hit. I just want to help the team win and if that means batting down in the order, that's fine."

New York Post Columnist Mike Vaccaro asked, "Is it true you are demanding a trade?"

"A trade? No, not at all. It hasn't crossed my mind," the smiling Bramage said. "I enjoy playing here. I came up through the system here. I can't imagine playing for another team. So no, I haven't asked for a trade. I hope to play here my entire career."

"Dane, are you and Namovicz getting along?" asked long-time baseball analyst Tony DeMarco.

"Me and Namo? Of course we're getting along. I respect him not only as a great manager, but as a great person. Where you guys get all this stuff I'll never know. I have to go get ready. We have a game to win tonight."

Several minutes later, the disturbing sounds of a water cooler being beaten to smithereens by a bat was heard coming from the nearby indoor batting cage.

Apparently, Dane Bramage was not in the lineup that night.

KAZAKHSTANI SPORTS TALK FAILS

The first, and apparently last, all-sports radio station catering to Kazakhstanies in the United States has folded.

"I, along with my investors, thought that an all-sports radio station for Kazakhstani sporting enthusiasts could not possibly fail," said station owner and general manager Barmak Ruslatan. "With all the immigrants from Kazakhstan in New York I am baffled how it didn't work out."

Program director Nazar Bayevinlakam said, "We thought we had the programming in place to not only pacify the Kazakhstani people, but to also capture the American market. I don't understand how we could lose like this."

WKZK failed to register a single ratings point or generate one paid commercial spot in its two years on the air.

"We covered camel racing, chess, boxing, soccer and cross country skiing." Ruslatan added. "Looking back I'd have to blame soccer for our invisible ratings. At the end we tried to lure Dmitri "Mad Dog" Ibraimov, the best sport talker in Kazakhstan to come to New York and salvage our station, but he wouldn't come to a country that didn't have his favorite sport—Ostrich racing."

WKZK has been sold to Stanislav Dombrowski who plans to change the format to 'All Polka All The Time.'

"Polka is making a comeback and we are going to ride the wave baby," explained Dombrowski.

In the meantime, hundreds of cab drivers in New York City are once again deprived of riveting Kazakhstani related sports talk.

THE BOOSTER

Prominent Nashville businessman Percival "Bobby" Dillenbrand has been barred from Vanderbilt University sporting events and banned from having contact with Commodore athletes.

Dillenbrand, who wanted to become a "super booster" for the school, was accused of trying to give cars to recruits and cash gifts to current student-athletes who excelled on the field of play.

"Vandy told me they play by the rules," rued Dillenbrand. "I asked them, did y'all know this is the SEC?"

Dillenbrand, owner of the popular "Bobby D's BBQ" chain of restaurants, was hoping to help Vanderbilt move into the upper echelon of the Southeastern Conference. Instead, he only drew the wrath of Vandy administrators.

"We want no part of Dillenbrand," said associate athletic director Cheryl Petticoat. "He's bad news. We don't want to be put on probation or damage our reputation."

Dillenbrand, who never attended college, but grew an affinity for Vandy sports said, "With all the budget constraints and cutbacks these days you would think they would want a booster of my caliber. I guess Vanderbilt doesn't want millions of dollars to filter into their athletic program. I suppose they don't want the blue chip athletes that take handouts like at other schools that win National Championships. It pains me to say that I'll have to become a booster at another school."

Within minutes of hearing his comments, Dillenbrand entertained a phone call from Alabama football coach Nick Saban. Several other football and basketball coaches in the SEC also placed calls to Dillenbrand.

"We would welcome Bobby's support of Bama athletics," said Saban. "He loves college sports and if Vandy doesn't want him, we would love for him to become part of the Crimson Tide family."

When reminded of Dillenbrand's shady past, Saban said to a reporter, "Come on now, why y'all have to bring that up? Come on, let's get a bite to eat. How about some barbeque at Bobby D's? Hey, pick a number, any number, from one to ten."

"Six," said the reporter.

"Wrong," said Saban. "It was two. You're buying buddy."

THIS DATE IN BASKETBALL HISTORY

When basketball was invented in 1891 by Doctor James Naismith in Springfield, Massachusetts the goal was literally a peach basket. After each score, an official would climb up a ladder to retrieve the ball. This slowed the game down considerably.

Twelve years later, Wilber Traxler, a basketball official and native of Erie, Pennsylvania, modified the peach basket and thereby altered the game of basketball forever.

On that 25th day of February in 1903, Traxler, who was getting tired of climbing a ladder all day to get the ball, had a sudden vision.

"I thought, why not cut a hole in the bottom of the peach basket?" Traxler told the Sporting News in a 1924 interview. "This would speed up the game, making it unnecessary for me to climb up and down the ladder to get the ball. It seemed like a prudent thing to do."

Traxler's innovation, while putting an untold number of ball retrievers out of work, did quicken the pace of game and help make basketball the fast, exciting spectacle it is today.

"We are indebted to Wilbur's wonderful contribution to our game," said NBA Commissioner David Stern, "but it's not like somebody wouldn't have cut a hole in the bottom of the peach basket sooner or later."

Stern took a deep breath, tapped his fingers on his credenza and continued. "To be honest, Traxler gets a little too much credit if you ask me. Without him do you think we would still be getting basketballs out of a peach basket?

But you wanted me to say something nice, so I did. Now if you'll excuse me I have to think about something nice to say about Richard Lugendorf, the inventor of the sweatband."

DOMINICAN MYSTERY

Dominican's are very good in baseball, but not so good at hockey. This, according to a recent study conducted by the William D. Jones Institute of Societal Research.

"This was an intriguing study," said lead researcher Lars Lifrak. "We know people from the Dominican Republic are athletically gifted. Just look at any Major League baseball roster. Yet scanning the rosters of NHL teams there are hardly any Dominican players. Why?"

Assistant project researcher Daniela Garrity added, "Actually, there are no Dominican's in the NHL. Not one."

"It is quite a mystery when you think about it," said Lifrak as he adjusted his bow tie.

"Mystery?" said Garrity. "Yeah, some mystery. I'm guessing because there isn't one ice rink in the Dominican Republic and the fact that people there can't afford hockey equipment anyway, probably has something to do with it. And it's always 95-degrees and Dominican's are absolutely in love with baseball. Well, that might just might be a factor. Or maybe I'm missing something."

Lifrak shot a stern look at his assistant. "OK, that's enough Daniela," said Lifrak. "I think you need to get back to your other project on why midgets suck at basketball."

STEPPING STONE

Heather Sundlin held her breath along with the other ten candidates. There were only four openings and the moment of truth was here.

When Heather heard her name called she was nearly overcome with joy.

"Oh my God," shrieked Heather. "I can't believe it. I'm a Philadelphia Eagles cheerleader!"

Sundlin had practiced and trained for months preparing for the grueling Eagles cheerleader tryouts. She made it, but she wasn't about to stop there.

"Being an Eagles cheerleader is great and all," said Heather, "but it's just a stepping stone to my true career goal of becoming an exotic dancer!"

THE JASPER STORY

Jasper Dunninger was born four months prematurely in Niles, Michigan. Doctors didn't think he'd make it. He did.

As a child, Jasper was afflicted with polio. He overcame it. In high school, Jasper was thought to be stupid. He wasn't. He was, however, diagnosed with dyslexia which he also defeated.

Not a large boy, Jasper gravitated towards running. He didn't have many friends and found the solitude of long-distance running refreshing, energizing and therapeutic.

After an uneventful cross country track career at Niles High, Jasper enrolled at Manchester College, a small school in Indiana to continue his running career.

He thought he'd get a degree in philosophy or some other worthless field and then go back to Niles and work for the next forty years or so. Maybe raise a family. The future didn't look bright for Jasper.

Well, Jasper did get a degree from Manchester College. But much to his surprise, his running career took off. It was the one thing in life he liked and he became the best cross country runner in school history.

Jasper continued to run after graduating. He ran in a few marathons and did alright. Then he learned the U. S. Olympic team was holding time trials in Los Angeles.

Why not?

Jasper entered and finished fourth. He was proud to be an alternate on the United States Olympic team. Not bad for a kid that nobody in Niles thought would amount to anything. Characteristically, there wasn't even a mention about Jasper's feat in the local newspapers.

A week before the Olympic team was to head to Beijing, China, Jasper got a call from Coach Alan Terry.

"Jasper, you in shape?"

"Absolutely. I've been training harder than I ever have," replied Dunninger.

"Great. You're on the team. Lucas was caught with crack and a prostitute. He's done. We fly out next week."

The nobody from Niles, Michigan was now on the United States Olympic Team. Jasper was in shock. He was now the most famous person to come out of Niles, Michigan since, well since some radio guy named Moller years earlier.

Jasper was a long-shot to medal in the Olympic Marathon. The Kenyans dominated the event. He wasn't even the best on his own team. Yet Jasper, since day one, always seemed to beat the odds.

Jasper Dunninger ran the race of his life. As he entered Beijing National Stadium, he was in second place, about twenty yards behind Kenya's Samuel Wanjiru.

With the crowd screaming, Dunninger was gaining on Wanjiru. As he was closing, Wanjiru broke the tape just two seconds ahead of the game American.

Jasper would have to settle for the Silver medal. He was never more proud in his life.

On the long plane ride back to the states, Jasper thought about the race. He wasn't upset at all. He gave it his absolute best and came up short to a great runner. He also thought about the reception he would get when he returned to Niles. A parade probably. The key to the city. Speaking engagements. The future never looked better for Jasper Dunninger.

Upon arrival, there was no welcoming committee for Jasper. No banners, no parade. Nothing. He picked up the paper, *"The Niles Star."* A small headline on the second page of the sports section read, "Olympic Loser Returns Home."

It seemed as if nobody in Niles cared about Jasper Dunninger. It was as if he was still the awkward, lonely kid. Even his overbearing dad was disappointed that Jasper came in second and only got the Silver medal.

But a funny thing happened to the misfit from Michigan. He made an appearance on the Tonight Show with Jay Leno. A book was written about his life story and made into a major motion picture. Speaking engagements from all across the country started coming his way. Jasper was now famous and wealthy with a beautiful girlfriend to boot. The only thing he didn't have? The phone numbers of anyone from Niles, Michigan.

THE GUEST SPEAKER

The students at Lincoln Elementary School in Pittsburgh were excited when they were told a guest speaker from the Pirates would be paying them a visit.

It was always a fun day for the kids when a speaker would show up. They were taught by the teachers to be respectful and to have questions ready.

The special guest was Pirates bullpen coach Mike Pressler. A former minor leaguer, Pressler was eager to meet the students and tell them all about his job.

After twenty minutes of describing his duties, Pressler opened up the floor for a question and answer session.

"So you answer the phone in the bullpen?" asked Silvia Wicks.

"Yes. The manager tells me who to get warmed up," replied Pressler.

"Can't one of the pitchers answer the phone?" wondered Freddie Frazier.

"Well, um, no, that's my job."

"You said that you reach into the ball bag and hand the pitchers a baseball to warm up," said Barry Steckel. "Why can't the pitcher get the ball himself?"

"You see, that is what the Pirates hired me to do," said the coach who was trying to remain calm.

"One of your responsibilities is to make sure there are rosin bags on the bullpen mounds," said Mike Sramac.

"That is correct."

"How come the bat boy or the groundskeeper doesn't take care of that?" Sramac questioned.

"Yeah," many of the kids said.

"Well, that's my job. Ok. That's what I do," replied the clearly agitated Pressler.

The grilling continued.

"Do you need to have an education to be a bullpen coach?" Ashley Estenor wanted to know.

"Well, actually, ah, no."

"We had a policeman here last week to talk to us," Ronnie Zolanski said. "THAT seems like a really tough and important job."

Pressler finally snapped. "Look, I never said it was a hard job. I know a chimp could do my job but what the hell are you kids trying to do, get me fired? I had a bunch of free tickets and some caps to give out but not now. You want to bust my balls? Screw you, you little bastards. I'm out of here!"

It would likely be a long time until a member of the Pirates would speak again at Lincoln Elementary school in Pittsburgh.

UP TO HIS "OLD" TRICKS

Danny Almonte, the left-handed pitcher who dominated in the 2001 Little League World Series—due to the fact that he was two years older than the competition, has been embroiled in another baseball related scandal.

Almonte, 23, has been caught pitching in a 50 and over senior baseball league.

"We thought this guy looked youthful," said league commissioner Bart Sydler. "He was just dominating the old fat guys, but we couldn't do anything about it since his birth certificate and driver's license indicated he was 53."

After authorities responded to complaints from several players, an investigation revealed the hoax.

"We thought he looked a little young," said Arnie Burnbaum, 57. "He was throwing ninety miles per hour. We don't get many guys in our league who can do that. Actually, nobody in our league can do that. Although when Sandy Koufax threw out the first pitch two years ago at our national tournament he hit ninety-three on the radar gun."

Almonte proclaimed his innocence and blamed any mix-up on poor record keeping from officials in the Dominican Republic, his birthplace.

"I'm 53, honest," said Almonte. "I have that rare anti-aging disease so while it may look like I'm 23, I'm really in my fifties."

Almonte will have to return his MVP award and has been banned from senior league competition.

"That's alright," the unfazed Almonte responded. "There's a girls sixteen through eighteen-year-old softball league I'm working on joining. If anyone can pull it off it's me."

A LOVE STORY

Paul Nichols was taking a stroll down the 16th Street Mall in Denver on his lunch break. Approaching him, walking in the opposite direction on this sunny May day, was Jennifer Riley, also on her lunch break.

Paul simply thought, "Wow!"

Jennifer thought, "He's good looking. Probably taken though."

When Jennifer passed by, Paul looked back to get another view. Jennifer did the same and they shared an embarrassing smile and continued on their way.

Paul thought about Jennifer all day, an attractive, shapely blonde with an amazing smile. Why hadn't he said something to her? He was kicking himself.

Jennifer couldn't concentrate at work. She couldn't get Paul out of her mind.

The next day, same time and place at the mall, Paul was hoping to see the fetching Jennifer. To his surprise and delight, Jennifer walked up to him and said hello. They chatted, and chatted some more. They exchanged numbers and both were late getting back to work.

They dated for five weeks and loved every minute of it. Dinners, movies, a trip to the zoo, the art museum. And, of course, the magical kisses. It was wonderful.

Paul, a huge sports fan, refrained from talking about sports since he didn't want to scare Jennifer away. He knew that sometimes women feel they come in second to sports. Jennifer, also a big sports fan, found it refreshing that she found a guy who didn't talk only about sports.

Jennifer finally found the nerve to say, "I love you Paul."

Paul was joyous. He replied, "I love you too Jennifer."

"My parents would like to meet you," said Jennifer. "I've told them all about you."

"I want to meet them too."

On Friday evening, Paul, wearing a suit and tie and with flowers for Jennifer and her mother, showed up to meet the family. He was confident he would like Jenn's folks. She was absolutely wonderful, so surely the rest of the family was awesome too.

Upon arrival at the Riley household, Paul took a deep breath, grabbed the flowers and walked up to the front door and rang the bell.

Jennifer answered, invited Paul in and gave him a big hug. Then she introduced him to her parents.

After exchanging pleasantries, Paul looked around the living room. There were Oakland Raiders pictures on the walls. Her younger brother was wearing a Raiders jersey. There was a replica Raiders helmet on a shelf. A biography of Al Davis was on the coffee table.

He then saw a picture of Jennifer with former Raiders quarterback Kenny Stabler, his arm draped over her shoulders.

Paul stood silent for a moment. He began to get misty-eyed. He looked at Jennifer.
"How could you?" he demanded. "How could you do this to me?" He then slammed the flowers on the floor and headed for the door, shoving her little brother into the wall and kicking their dog Plunkett in the process.

Paul Nichols was heartbroken. The girl of his dreams was a Raiders fan. No self-respecting Denver Broncos fan could ever continue a relationship with such a sick and twisted individual.

THE NO CHANCE
PERSONAL AD

I'm a 32-year-old, overweight (working on it), short, balding white male who enjoys playing fantasy football, fantasy baseball, fantasy hockey, fantasy basketball and fantasy soccer.

My other interests include ice fishing, playing chess, watching sports on television, collecting sports memorabilia, attending baseball card shows, listening to sports talk radio, internet pornography, bowling, playing softball (4 leagues!) and long walks on the beach. I am also a fast food connoisseur.

I'm looking for an extremely attractive woman with similar interests for romantic good times. No fatties please. I am employed as an assistant retail manager for a local sporting goods outlet. Please reply to: harveythestud@yahoo.com.

FLEMING THE ODDBALL

In a sport which is known for having a multitude of superstitious players, Brian Fleming is referred to as the most superstitious man in baseball. Now in his fifth season, the Mariners utility infielder even makes his teammates shake their heads.

"Brian is a nutcase," said Seattle pitcher Greg Sapakoff. "Even by baseball standards the guy should be locked up."

Some of his superstitions include eating the same meal of oatmeal, chicken, pasta, green beans and rice three times a day, every day throughout the season. He must wear the same underwear and socks every day, although he will wash them twice a week. He never watches National League highlights on ESPN. He will always say "Hi Jerry" to the home plate umpire, no matter what the umpire's name is. He'll sit in the same spot in the dugout, on the team bus and plane. And he always waits 11 minutes in the hotel lobby after getting his room key. He's learning how to speak Swahili, just in case, and carries a clarinet with him on road trips, although he can't play it. Those are just a few of Fleming's superstitions.

"I wouldn't call them superstitions," said Fleming. "I would call them rituals. Everyone knows it's bad luck to be superstitious."

While his teammates accept Fleming's quirky behavior, right fielder Ichiro Suzuki says, "Yes, Brian has all these ridiculous superstitions. Why? The guy is a lifetime .217 hitter. I think he needs some new superstitions—like mixing in a few hits."

THE PROPOSAL

Mark Kramer adjusted his tie. He looked into the restroom mirror. He was nervous, but confident. His hair was neat and his shoes polished. Mark rejoined his business partner Ken Schwartz in the ESPN waiting room.

"Mr. Bodenheimer will see you now," said the receptionist.

After months of trying to arrange a meeting with the president of ESPN, Mark and Ken were excited to finally have the opportunity to make their pitch.

"It's show time," whispered Mark to Ken.

They entered the conference room. George Bodenheimer, and several other ESPN decision makers, were sitting at a large mahogany table.

For the next hour, Mark and Ken proceeded to passionately make their case as to why ESPN should become the new exclusive home of the recently formed United States Wiffleball League, or USWBL.

"Wiffleball is an American institution," continued Mark. "Everybody has played the sport at one time or another. People love Wiffleball and our extensive market research shows people will definitely watch the sport on television." He looked at Ken.

"This could be a gold mine for ESPN," Ken added enthusiastically.

Intrigued by the possibility of Wiffleball on ESPN, the executives began to edge forward in their seats.

The presentation was going smoothly, better than Mark and Ken had anticipated. A television deal with ESPN would cement the foundation of the USWBL. They had the owners and the players and now all they needed was that

TV contract. It was close to becoming a reality. It was up to Ken to close the presentation.

"So there you have it gentlemen, an opportunity for the USWBL and ESPN to become partners in this venture. To be honest with you, how could you not jump aboard on this opportunity? After all, have you seen some of the crappy programming you guys have on now. Billiards? PTI? Women's basketball? Soccer? Lumberjacking? Around The Horn? Come on, who the hell watches that crap? If it were up to me, there would be some people in here dusting off their resumes."

Mark got close to Ken and whispered, "No Ken, don't go there. Just wrap it up."

Ken was on a roll though. "Furthermore, if you don't come aboard right this very minute, we're taking this proposal to Fox Sports and you guys will be wondering how you could be so stupid. So, where are the papers? Let's sign this puppy now. It's a no-brainer."

In the rental car, heading towards the Hartford airport, Ken wondered, "Why do you think we got turned down?"

Mark pulled the car onto the shoulder of Interstate 91. His grip tightened around the steering wheel. He then uttered his first words since the conclusion of the meeting. "Get out!"

WORLD RECORD HOLDER

Les Grantham always dreamed of being an athlete. He tried his best, but he was far from being athletically gifted. But Les was a stubborn sort, so he decided he needed to come up with a plan that would get him recognized as a notable athlete.

One afternoon while relaxing on his front porch, it came to him. He could be the world record holder in The Mini-Triathlon!

Les asked his neighbor Steve if he could use his swimming pool.

Check.

Then he needed to map out a half-mile running course that wound through the neighborhood.

Check.

Then a lap around the block on a bike would complete the Mini-Triathlon.

Les gathered some of his buddies and explained the Mini-Triathlon.

The Saturday morning cloud cover lifted and it was a perfect day for the first annual Kenosha, Wisconsin Mini-Triathlon.

Les was the first competitor.

He dove into Steve's pool and swam forty feet to the other side in a respectable eleven seconds. He exited the pool quickly and put on his running shoes. He completed the half-mile run in 6:45. Then he jumped on the bike and furiously pedaled around the block in 3:21.

He completed the Mini-Triathlon in 10:17, a new world record!

Of the seven other contestants entered in the Mini-Triathlon, Les Grantham finished last.

There were no TV cameras or newspaper reporters to record the event. But for a few glorious moments, even though nobody else knew it, Les was a world record holding athlete.

Mission accomplished.

TYSON VS. TYSON

"I spent ten years in the major leagues and now I can't even get a job," lamented former Cardinals and Cubs infielder Mike Tyson. "All because of that guy."

That guy that Tyson is referring to is former heavyweight champeen, Mike Tyson.

"He's done nothing but besmirch my name over the years and I've had it. Things were great when I was the only Mike Tyson, then that jackass had to ruin everything for me."

The former baseball player constantly has creditors looking for money from him. He has to hear all the jokes and snide comments. He's been turned down for home and car loans. He has drunks continually challenge him to fights and he was even accused of stealing the boxer's identity.

"He's the last guy whose identity I would steal," said the baseball Tyson. "I worked hard to build a career in and out of baseball, but every time someone learns of my name, they immediately think I'm the boxer."

He began to get agitated. "Look, I'm white and 59-years-old. Plus I don't have a facial tattoo. But that still doesn't convince people I'm not the boxer Mike Tyson."

Why doesn't the former baseball player change his name?

"I've thought about it," Tyson said, "but my top choices of Pacman Jones, Terrell Owens, John Daly and Travis Henry were all nixed by my lawyer. I have no recourse left but to sue my namesake."

When told the baseball Mike Tyson was suing him for ruining his good reputation, the boxing Tyson said, "He's suing me? I should sue him. The guy was a .241 lifetime hitter. He's made MY life miserable."

BRONX SWEATSHOP

Michael Green and Raphael Rivas are threatening to go on strike from their jobs as batboys for the New York Yankees.

Agent Ron Del Duca, representing the pair of 13-year-olds, said, "Mikey and Ralphie both work their asses off for the Yankees, above and beyond the call of duty. Not only are the Yankees violating child labor laws, they are, you know, violating child labor laws."

"I asked if I could leave after the seventh inning so I could get home and get to bed so I can get to school the next day." Green said. "But they said no, I have to vacuum the clubhouse after games. What can I do, my dad won't let me quit."

Rivas tells the harrowing story of being abused by third baseman Alex Rodriguez. "A-Rod thinks I'm his personal flunky boy. Get me a sandwich. Get me a pen. Get me something to drink. Put Madonna on the pass list. Shine my shoes. It gets tiresome. I just want to get the bats and put baseballs in the ball bag. That's my job description, but like Mikey, my mom and dad won't let me quit."

When Hal Steinbrenner was questioned about the alleged sweatshop the team was running, the Yankees owner said, "I told the kids to quit if they didn't like it. Their parents don't seem to mind. Maybe it's because I pay those punk kids two-million a year. Let's see them get that from the Mets."

CELEBRITY BOXING

In a wild bout between 70's television icons, Florence Henderson, of *"The Brady Bunch"* knocked out Valerie Harper of *"The Mary Tyler Moore Show"* to capture the senior division title of the MGM Grand Hotel and Casino Celebrity Boxing Tournament in Las Vegas.

"They said I couldn't do it since Harper is six years younger than me," crowed Henderson in her post fight interview. "Now bring on that Partridge kid. I'll kick his (bleeping) ass!"

Henderson, 75, was referring to Danny Bonaduce who parlayed his child acting gig on *The Partridge Family* into nothing and then a celebrity boxing career.

Bonaduce said, "I want no part of Florence. She used to beat the crap out of my TV mom Shirley Jones, not only in the studio parking lot, but in the ratings too. She's one tough mama."

Bonaduce was slated to face D-list celebrity Gary Coleman of *Diff'rent Strokes* fame, in a celebrity boxing match last month in Frankfort, Kentucky; however, the fight had to be cancelled due to Coleman's untimely death.

"It's too bad that Gary died. I would have had the reach advantage on Coleman so I know I would have whipped his butt. Plus, he had a couple of kidney transplants which also would have helped me. Rest in peace Gary. Now I want his TV brother, that jackass Todd Bridges."

After hearing this, Henderson said, "That Bonadouchebag is fighting Bridges? He's ducking me, that rat bastard."

THE NBA'S GREATEST
ACCORDING TO DUKE

It may surprise some that David Duke, a white nationalist and former Grand Wizard of the Ku Klux Klan, is a huge sports fan particularly of the NBA.

"Even though some see me as a racist, I look at sports as the ultimate level playing field," said Duke. "Skin color has nothing to do with competing in sports."

Duke, no relation to the great professional bowler Norm Duke, has followed the NBA since he was a child and many consider him to be an expert on the game.

"I love the college game, but the NBA is where the greatest athletes in the world play," said the controversial figure.

Duke recently wrote a book on basketball that listed his greatest players in NBA history.

"My first team all-NBA squad consists of John Stockton at the point. Jerry West would be my shooting guard. I went with Bill Walton at center and my forwards are Larry Bird and Kevin McHale," said Duke. "My second team consists of Steve Nash at point guard. Pistol Pete Maravich is the shooting guard. At center I'm going with the vastly underrated Dave Cowens. The forwards would be Rick Barry and Dollar Bill Bradley."

Duke also included an honorable mention team consisting of guards Bob Cousy and John "Hondo" Havlicek, center George Mikan and forwards Dirk Nowitzki and Dave DeBusschere. Duke added it was tough keeping guys like Tom Chambers, Billy Cunningham, Steve Kerr, John Paxson and Bill Laimbeer off the list.

When asked why Michael Jordan, Kareem Abdul-Jabbar, Julius Erving, Karl Malone, Oscar Robertson, Charles Barkley, and Magic Johnson didn't make the cut, Duke said, "Tough choices had to be made. I gave them careful, painstaking consideration. But it boiled down to the fact that while very good players, they just didn't have the intangibles to crack my all-time top fifteen."

THE SMARTEST RECRUIT

Oliver Fisher was the smartest kid ever in the long and glorious history of Spring Valley High School in New York. He never posted less than an A in any class and recorded a perfect score on the SAT. His IQ was an off the charts 163. Simply put, he was a genius.

Every Ivy League institution wanted the highly intelligent Fisher to matriculate at their school. He also had offers from MIT, RPI, West Point and Oxford. The future certainly looked bright for the mentally gifted scholar.

Even though he wasn't an athlete, the entire student body at Spring Valley was anxious to see where the affable Fisher would go to school. The whole county and state was eager to learn of his choice.

Fisher agreed to the administration's request that he make his announcement in the gymnasium before the entire junior and senior classes.

The media assembled, the gym was packed and Fisher, the academic whiz kid, walked calmly to the podium.

"First off, I'd like to thank my parents for giving me support and guidance all these years. Thank you to all my classmates and to my wonderful teachers here at Spring Valley," said Fisher. "I am ready to announce where I will go to college."

There were four hats on the podium: Yale, Harvard, Princeton and MIT. The tension in the gym was thicker than the lenses of Fisher's glasses.

After a few tense moments, Fisher, displaying the showmanship that his parents never knew he had, reached down below the podium. He grabbed a hat and put it on his head.

The hat read, "Alabama Crimson Tide."

As Fisher wore the hat proudly, his mother fainted and his father stormed out of the gym.

Representatives from Yale, Harvard, Princeton and MIT were stunned at the young man's decision.

"I seriously considered the Ivy League and other brainiac schools, but to be honest the football played by those schools suck," explained Fisher. "Alabama has everything I want in a school. A tradition-laden football team in a great conference with a multitude of hot chicks. When I land that elusive first date, she's sure to be a babe. Plus, by not going the 'academic school' route, I'll be the smartest kid in school again. I won't even have to go to class. Finally, since sports wagering is huge in Alabama, I can set up that online gambling syndicate that caters to rich college kids with that new software I developed. Football, babes, wealth, I'll have it all in Tuscaloosa!"

Yes, Oliver Fisher was the smartest kid ever.

THE CELEBRATION

After Michigan State won the Alamo Bowl over Nebraska, 24-14, Spartan fans back in East Lansing were in an uproarious mood.

No one was more jacked up than Clint Mulrooney. The long-time Spartan fan ran out of Champions Sports Bar and Grill and joined the celebration with hundreds of other die-hard Spartans fans.

Of course the joyous crowd lit bonfires and threw bricks through store fronts. That is to be expected these days, especially in East Lansing.

As they turned down Trowbridge Road, the increasingly hostile crowd began to vandalize homes and create mayhem.

The inebriated Mulrooney was having the time of his life. He took a Molotov Cocktail and tossed it through the window of a nicely kept home. Then he and several other miscreants overturned the car in the driveway and smashed all the lawn ornaments.

Soon a police cruiser rounded up the drunkards and took them to the drunk tank.

Once the unruly bunch sobered up, they were issued summonses and a court date.
Mulrooney was embarrassed by his behavior although he didn't recall too much of it.

As he walked down the block to his home he was bewildered.

"What the hell happened to my house?" said Mulrooney to no one in particular. "My car, who overturned my car?"

Then it all came back to Mulrooney. He remembered

that he was the one who led the assault on his own home. How would he explain that to the insurance people?

"Damn, I thought I was torching my stupid neighbor's house," Mulrooney said. "You know, just for fun. I guess it isn't so funny now that I realize it's my house. Crap, look at that mess. But wait, THE SPARTANS WON DAMN IT, THE SPARTANS WON!!!"

BENCHED

Tyler Parnell was benched for yesterday's Lakewood Little League tilt between the Astros and White Sox.

Parnell, 10, the shortstop for the Astros was told to ride the pine by Head Coach Don Zellars.

"Tyler is our best player, but he refuses to engage in infield chatter," said Zellars. "All the other kids chatter, but Tyler seems more interested on focusing on his game instead of trying to rattle the opposing team. That's selfish and why he was benched. I'm in charge here."

Tyler wasn't happy with the benching.

"I looked forward to the game all week and then I'm told to take a seat. Why? Just because I won't yell 'swing batter swing' or 'we want a pitcher not a belly itcher' he puts me on the bench? What the (bleep) is a belly itcher anyway? All I know is when I make it to the majors Coach Zellars ain't getting no free tickets from me. They don't do that chatter crap in The Show."

SAVED

Following his Major League playing career, Bobby Carlson struggled in the real world. Without the structure of baseball, Carlson drifted from job to job and found it difficult to find something he could embrace.

His marriage was on the rocks and he felt worthless.

Former teammate Andy Holland suggested he get in touch with The Lord.

"I decided to take Andy's advice," said Carlson. "It was the best decision I've ever made."

Carlson met with a priest and started studying Christianity. His parents were devout Catholics and were happy to see their son finally connect with his religion.

Carlson's marriage is now as solid as it has ever been. He feels closer to his children. He works for a life insurance company and feels gratified to be helping people in such an important way.

"People need the right life insurance. Buy term and invest the difference is our philosophy," Carlson said. "I'm making an impact in their lives. It's all because I've embraced my Lord and Savior Jesus Christ."

He is, of course, eager to spread the gospel to those who need such guidance. Carlson says, "Now my life has purpose and meaning in such wonderful ways."

His former baseball manager Whitey Carruthers was happy that Carlson turned his life over to The Lord.

"Really? So Carlson found Jesus. Well ain't that grand? Too bad he didn't find Jesus 15 years ago. Then maybe he could have found a way to improve on that damn .243 batting average of his and I wouldn't have gotten fired."

JUMPING SHIP

"We's gonna punch his lights out," said Donnie Gaston, manager for middleweight contender Tony Barlotti. "We gots no doubt that when the fight ends, Tony and me will be raising our hands in triumph. We's gonna knock that bum out. We's been training hard and we's can't be stopped. I know we's the underdog, but me and Tony is gonna shock the world Saturday night. Bank on it. We's gonna be world champeens."

With those words, Gaston adjusted his pinky ring and walked away from the podium, refusing to take questions from the assembled media. All the confident manager would say is, "See me Saturday night."

Fast forward three days to Saturday evening in Las Vegas. ...

"What happened out there?" asked reporter Martin Lenz to boxing manager Donnie Gaston.

"I have no idea," replied Gaston. "The kid blew it. He messed up. He didn't do as he was told. He wouldn't listen or follow them directions. He's certainly finished. Tony didn't get in there and fight like he can and that's why he got knocked out. He just done blew a chance to become the champ." Gaston adjusted his pinky ring again. "Anyway, I want to tell you guys about a fighter I have on the rise. I'm gonna make him a champeen. We's gonna be unstoppable. ..."

THE SCRIPT

John Olander was ecstatic. His son's Pee Wee football team, the Dolphins, won the championship with a 12-6 win over the Rams. As the team celebrated on the field, Mr. Olander knew what he had to do.

A few weeks later, the movie script was complete. It was John's first screenplay and, although biased, he thought it was really good.

He showed the script to Dan Kitteridge, the dad of another player on the team.

"That's good John, real good," said Kitteridge. "This will make a hell of a movie."

That convinced Olander that it was time to take the script to a professional.

After weeks of trying to set up an appointment, Olander finally convinced veteran independent filmmaker Thomas Wells to take a look.

"So, I've read the script John," said Wells. "Let me get this straight. This Pee Wee football team won the championship of their league."

"That's correct," said Olander.

"Were there any dying kids on the team?

"Uh …no."

"Any kids with major physical handicaps?"

"No."

"Let's see. Was this a team of underdogs that somehow came together and miraculously won the championship."

"No. We expected to win."

"Was the coach getting it on with any of the player's moms?"

"God no, none of that."

"I see. Mmmmm. Well, let me ask you this John. What is special about this team?"

"We won the championship."

"There are five thousand Pee Wee football teams that won championships this year. I need something I can work with."

Several weeks later, after a re-write, Olander again met with Wells.

Wells looked over the premise page.

It read: '*A Pee Wee football team with an alcoholic quarterback and a pot smoking star running back, rally to win the championship despite the obnoxious head coach who is sleeping with several of the players mothers. One of the players is dying of lupus, another*
had a leg amputated and a third player has Down Syndrome. Throw in the assistant coach teaching the kids how to gamble, the team treasurer embezzling concessions profits, plus the bribery of referees and what you have is an uproarious and hilarious look at a team of lovable misfits and degenerates who conquer all.'

Wells took his glasses off. He sat there thinking. Then he looked at Olander and said, "Well, John, now I have something we can work with."

THE SPORTS AUTHORITY

The phone rang at 11:23 p.m.

It was Danny. "Matt, who was the American League Cy Young award winner in 1980?"

"Steve Stone," replied Matt McGurgan of Lincolnshire, Illinois.

"YEAH! Thanks Matt," said Danny who then hung up.

Fifteen minutes later, Greg called. "Hey Matt, tell me, which team won the Stanley
Cup in 1989 and in how many games?"

It took Matt all of two seconds to reply, "Calgary Flames, 6 games."

"Damn. I thought it was Montreal ," said Greg. "Hey, thanks anyway Matt."

This scenario played out several more times that evening, denying Matt of precious sleep.

"I'm cursed," Matt said. "I have this abundance of sports knowledge and my friends always call me up to win bar bets. I'm their living breathing sports encyclopedia. At one time I wanted to be a doctor (long pause), but I guess this is my contribution to society. Sad isn't it?"

What is also sad is that it appears all of Matt's friends are degenerate gamblers and alcoholics. Yes, it's a lonely world out there for sports savants.

EXPERIMENT GONE BAD

It was just an exhibition game, but the final score indicated that Bud Selig's plan to follow the steroid era of baseball with the aluminum bat era would likely not come to fruition.

On a warm March day in Tempe, Arizona, with both teams using aluminum bats, the Angels clobbered the Brewers 88-72 in a game that featured an unofficial spring training record of 57 home runs hit combined.

"I was open to the idea of experimenting with aluminum bats," said Angels Manager Mike Scioscia. "But after the Brewers jumped out to a 15-12 first inning lead, I began to think this wasn't such a good idea after all."

Commissioner Selig explained his rational for the experiment of using aluminum bats instead of wood.

"The steroid era was a wonderful time for baseball. Home runs sailing out of ballparks at an historical rate brought fans to the game. People loved watching guys like Bret Boone hit thirty-plus homers instead of his usual four."

Selig paused and offered a slight smile at the memory. He then continued. "After the do-gooders put an end to the steroid era we needed to find an alternative, so I thought let's try aluminum bats, which are basically bats on steroids."

Following the exhibition game, Angel's pitcher Jered Weaver was against aluminum bats in professional baseball. "I'd say let's stay with wood. Maybe the fact I gave up 7 home runs in the first inning and nearly had my head taken off with a line drive that ended up going over the center field fence has something to do with it. Now I have a spring ERA of 63.00 and I'm not sure if I'll make the ball club," said Weaver.

But the hitters, however, seemed to enjoy swinging with aluminum.

"I don't see a problem with it," said Brewers utility infielder Craig Counsell, who was 11-15 in the game with 6 homers and 17 RBI's. "I think this is a great idea by the commissioner. It would save trees from getting chopped down, which is good for the environment. Plus, it would certainly extend my career. Shoot, I have 35 career homers in 14 seasons. With aluminum I could double my career home run total in two months. Aluminum bats? Hell yeah, count me in!"

The commissioner has tabled his plan for the continued use of aluminum bats after watching the exhibition tilt.

"I still think it's a good idea," said Selig, "But we need to tinker with it since the game seemed to get a little out of hand. But it was exciting!"

THE CREDENTIAL

Veteran newspaper reporter Paul Dobbins always thought it was a double standard that female sports journalists were allowed into men's locker rooms, but male reporters were forbidden to enter a women's locker room.

"If I cover a female sporting event I'll need locker room access to do my job properly," said Dobbins. "This is discrimination and I'm going to fight it."

Sure enough, after complaining long and loud, Dobbins received an all-access press credential to a Los Angeles Sparks-Washington Mystics WNBA game.

Following the Saturday afternoon tilt, Dobbins ventured into the Mystics locker room to grab some quotes. What he saw may scar Dobbins for life.

"I walked in and when I turned the corner to the locker room area I saw several naked women," said Dobbins. "At least I think they were women. My eyes started burning and I had to get out of there. What was I thinking?"

Dobbins said he will no longer cover WNBA games, with one possible exception.

"Well, if Maria Sharapova ever becomes a WNBA player, I might apply for another press credential."

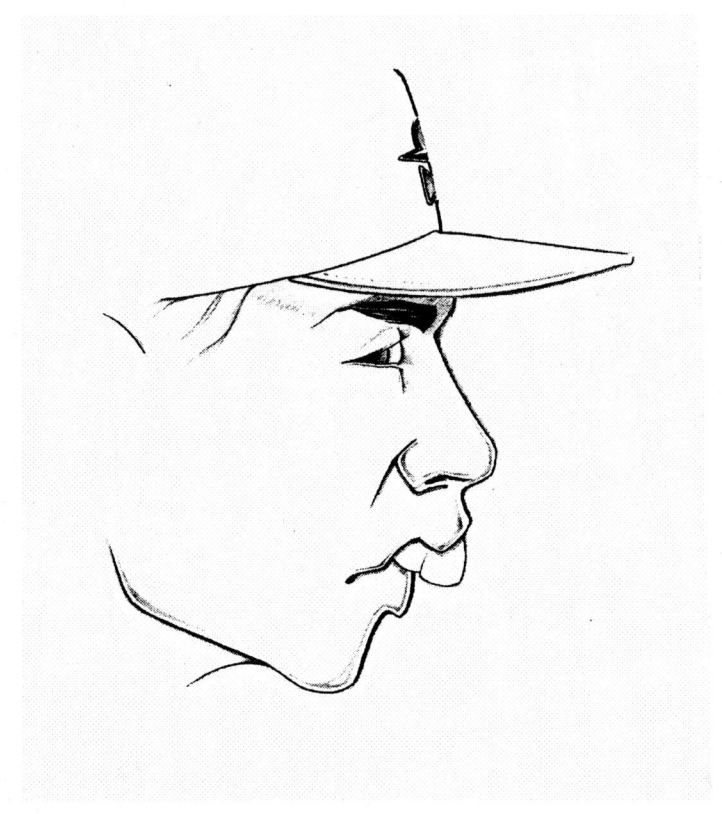

THE BOX OFFICE IS CLOSED

The phone rang in room 627 of the Grand Hyatt Hotel in New York City. Mariners rookie shortstop Tyler Parnell answered.

"Hello?"

"Tyler?"

"Yeah."

"It's me, Coach Zellars."

"Who?"

"Coach Zellars. I coached you in little league."

"Um, yeah. I remember. That was a long time ago."

"Yeah, like 14 years or so. How you doing Tyler?"

"Good. How about you?"

"Doing well. I'm here in New York for a family vacation. Say, I was wondering, can you get me a couple of tickets for the game tonight?"

"No, I can't do that."

"Really? I thought players get comp tickets."

"We do. Tell you what, why don't you ask one of your former players who yelled infield chatter all the time and made it to the big leagues to give you some tickets."

"But I thought that (click) ...Tyler? You there Tyler?"

Let this be a lesson to baseball managers everywhere. You don't bench Tyler Parnell.

DAVE THE IRREPRESSIBLE

Dave Cihla always maintained a positive attitude, even though he had a crummy job delivering bread and pastries at the Rosario Baking Company of Chicago.

Always an optimist, he didn't mind getting up at 4 a.m. for his early morning shift.

In the middle of his shift, on this particular Tuesday morning, Cihla was summoned into the manager's office and received bad news. His position had been eliminated and he was terminated immediately.

Actually, most people would think it was bad news, but not Dave.

"This is great news," exclaimed an excited Cihla.

"Now I have more time to get to Wrigley Field to catch the Cubs! This is our year you know!"

THE LIFER

Tom Buskirk recalled his first little league game. "I was so happy to put on the uniform and play such a great game. I remember crying when we got rained out. Actually, that happened last week."

Yes, Buskirk was rained out last week. The 53-year-old car salesman still plays baseball in an over 35 league.

"Make sure you say baseball," reminds Buskirk to the reporter for the neighborhood weekly. "Not that softball crap."

Buskirk's wife Delores supports her husband's passion for playing the game, although she questions his sanity.

"Tommy's had double hip replacement surgery, left knee replacement surgery, his hamstrings are constantly torn, plus he has had elbow surgery. I don't know how many times he's torn a rotator cuff." She continued. "Oh yeah, his season was cut short last year with a blown out Achilles Tendon."

"Look, all the greats have had their share of injuries," said Buskirk. "I'm no different."

Delores couldn't help herself. "You're no different? Those "greats" made millions of dollars playing the game and had the good sense to get out before their bodies imploded. You're not one of the greats Tom. You're just some guy who can't give it up and has nothing better to do."

Tom stared at Delores with a look of shock and disbelief. He then went into the bedroom. You could hear Tom sobbing behind the closed door. And it wasn't raining.

THE INTANGIBLES

Ray Hathaway was confident he had a great shot to land the job. After seventeen years of broadcasting experience in television and radio, the popular personality was ready for his career to take off.

The interview for a position as a sideline reporter for college football on ABC went well. The Vice President conducting the interview was dazzled by Ray's composure, experience, command of the language and his football knowledge. It was easily apparent that Ray would excel in this role. His keen insight would surely enhance the broadcasts.

Three weeks after the interview Ray received an encouraging call from an ABC producer. The job came down to Ray and another candidate.

"Between you and me Ray," said the producer, "you are the much more qualified candidate. It's just a matter of getting the paperwork done and final approval. I wouldn't worry if I were you."

Ray was excited. This was his big chance. He thought to himself, "It's true, hard work does indeed pay off."

A week later, Ray took a most crushing call. He didn't get the job after all. The other candidate got the job and had what the producer told Ray were "intangibles."

Two month's later, a still bummed out Ray decided to tune into ABC's season opening broadcast of the Miami-Florida State game.

Lead telecaster Brent Musberger said, "And now let's throw it down to our new side-line reporter Mandy Ferguson."

"It should be a great game Brent," began Mandy. "Um, these teams are rivals. Ah, also, it might rain tonight and, um, it might not. Um, back to you Brent."

Ray sat dumbfounded in his living room. He had lost out to a twenty-something bimbo with the intangibles Ray lacked—blonde hair, blue eyes and impressive 36-26-36 stats.

TIMMY THE INTENSE

Timmy was a young tennis prodigy. He seemed to have an excellent grasp of the game. His hand eye coordination was superior to most 8-year-olds. He was focused and determined, but had an unwavering temper.

It was at a National Tournament at the Connecticut Tennis Center in New Haven that Timmy's poor demeanor first came on display.

"Bullshit! That ball was IN asshole," screamed Timmy in his pint-sized voice after a close baseline call that went against him.

Throughout the match, young Timmy blurted out obscenities. Warnings from the chair umpire went unheeded.

Timmy's antics included racket abuse and kicking his chair during breaks. He even yelled at the crowd to, "Shut the hell up, I'm serving here."

Everybody in the audience was uncomfortable and appalled by the young boy's despicable behavior.

Well, almost everybody.

"Yeah, that's my boy! Way to go Timmy! Come on, kick some ass! Hey, that's my kid," said proud papa John McEnroe.

THE ARGUMENT

It was a close play at second, but Dodgers base runner Andre Ethier was called out by umpire Bob Davidson while trying to steal.

Dodgers Manager Joe Torre jumped out of the dugout and ran to second base to argue the call as the Los Angeles crowd voiced their displeasure.

"That was a terrible call Bob, just terrible," said the angry Torre. "He was safe."

Davidson let Torre vent for a few moments then said, "Joe, let me ask you a question. How close to the play was I?"

"About seven feet," said Torre.

"And was I in position to make the call Joe?"

"Yeah, you were."

"And let me ask you this Joe, how far from the play were you?"

"I don't know. About one-hundred twenty feet?"

"Sounds about right. So it is fair to say that I had a better look at it than you did?"

"Yeah, I'd say so."

"So Joe, another thing, in the history of baseball, which spans well over 100 years, has an umpire ever reversed a stolen base call at second base when the manager comes out to argue?"

"No. Come to think of it Bob, it's never happened."

"And Joe, you were expecting to be the first?"

"Well, yeah, I guess."

"Joe, would you agree you lost this argument?"

"Yeah, Bob. You win. Hey, how's the family?"

"Good. And yours?"

"Doing well, thanks. Well, time to get back to the dugout. Nice chatting with you Bob."

"You too Joe."

With that, another manager was no match for umpire Bob Davidson.

THE DINNER CONVERSATION

Keith Wolstenmeyer wanted to impress his dinner date.

"And I also play semi-pro baseball," he revealed.

Molly Bergen leaned forward. "Interesting. I'm not much into sports. If you don't mind, how much do you get paid?"

"I don't get paid anything," Keith replied.

"But you said it was semi-pro."

"Yes, it is semi-pro."

"Pro is short for professional, right?"

"Yes."

"Then you must get paid, right?"

"No. We actually have to pay the league for field rental, baseballs and umpires."

"But you said semi-pro, so you must get something, right? Otherwise you should be called amateurs."

"No, we don't get paid. I told you."

"Let me get this straight, you play semi-PRO baseball, but don't get paid. And you have to pay to play?"

"Correct."

"Does Derek Jeter get paid?"

"Of course. A lot too."

"So you could say he plays full-pro?"

"I guess you could say that. But he's in the majors and I'm just a semi-pro player."

"Why don't you play full-pro?"

"Because I play semi-pro."

"But wouldn't it be better to play full-pro instead of semi-pro."

"Yes it would, but I can't."

"Why not? That would make sense to me."

"Because I'm not good enough, OK? Does that make sense to you now?"

"You don't have to get upset about it Keith. A lot of people are semi-pro in something. They are usually called volunteers."

"Let's change the subject."

"Good idea. So, this is a nice restaurant. Thanks for bringing me here."

"Yes it is nice."

"Expensive I'm sure. Since you are a semi-pro baseball player how can you afford it? Will you need help with the bill?"

"No I don't need help with the bill. I have a job."

"What do you do?"

"I'm a social worker."

"Full-pro or semi-pro?"

"Do you want to leave?"

"That would be a good idea."

For some strange reason, Keith and Molly didn't have a second date.

THE FUTURE OF BASEBALL BROADCASTING

"Hi baseball fans and welcome to this afternoon's game between the Diamondbacks and Rockies at Coors Field. I'm Rick Glick and today's game is brought to you by ESurance, your online auto insurance outlet. Today's pitching match up, sponsored by Sprite ...obey your thirst ...has Brandon Webb going for Arizona and Ubaldo Jimenez for Colorado. Speaking of Colorado be sure to visit Colorado.com to plan your next Colorado vacation.

Webb comes into the game with a 6-2 record and an ERA of 3.41. And with Webb on the hill, this is a great time to remind you that the new Spiderman movie is currently in theaters now. Jimenez is completing his warm-up tosses, which gives me the chance to tell you to toss those dirty clothes in the washer and get them clean with Tide. The detergent that's soft on clothes but tough on dirt.

Jimenez is looking for his 4th win of the season. His era is a stingy 2.35. The right-hander ready to face Arizona leadoff hitter Stephen Drew. The first pitch brought to by Geico. So easy a Caveman can do it.

Drew steps in and here's the opening pitch by Jimenez—fastball for a called strike. And while you don't want to strikeout at the plate, you do want to strike out on the lanes. Visit Lucky Strike Lanes in Lakewood for the bowling experience of a lifetime. Jimenez deals. The 0-1 pitch, fouled back the screen. Remember fans to generously apply Coppertone all natural sunscreen, especially on hot sunny days like today. That's Coppertone, sun protection plus antioxidants.

The 0-2 pitch on the way, taken for a ball. And fans

you can have a ball at Water World. What a great way to cool off after the game. Water World is located in Federal Heights, just minutes north of downtown Denver. Jimenez gets the sign from Ianetta. This upcoming 1-2 pitch brought to you by Snickers.

Here it comes, swung on and fouled off into the upper deck on the first base side, near a fan that was snoozing. Fans, if you want a quality nap visit Mattress King for all your mattress needs. Drew steps back in the batters box, and if you need boxes, get them on the cheap at U-Haul. Makes moving a breeze. That's U-Haul. Here's another 1-2 offering by Jimenez, fastball low for ball two.

Jimenez hit ninety-seven miles per hour with that last pitch, and when you want speed, Metro Taxi is the service for you. Get's you where you want to go, fast.

The 2-2 pitch, swung on and it's a high fly ball to center, this flight of the baseball brought to you by our friends at Frontier Airlines. Fowler ambles in a few steps and makes the catch. And fans, you want to make sure to get your tickets to catch the Brewers when they come in this weekend. Tickets available at all Rockies dugout stores and King Soopers.

That brings up Diamondbacks third baseman Mark Reynolds, batting .276. Reynolds, a guy who gets the most out of his ability. Which leads us to the US Army. Join the Army today and be all you can be. Yes, we love all those who serve this fine country. Speaking of service, Tom Moller Buick in Littleton will give you the best customer service of any auto dealer anywhere. They guarantee it.

One out, nobody on, just underway here at Coors Field. No score. Jimenez fires to Reynolds. This pitch brought to you by Direct TV, inside for a ball. And fans, speaking of balls fans, a quick reminder that …"

THE TRANSCRIPT

Regina Delaney worked in the admissions department at West Virginia University in Morgantown. She couldn't help but laugh when she went over the transcript of Dewayne L. Mitchell from Chicago. It may have been the worst transcript she had ever seen in her fifteen years of work.

"Brad, check this out," Regina called to one of her colleagues.

Brad Carter took a look at the transcript. Mitchell was a D student and had a SAT score of just 430. He got 400 points for just signing his name. In addition to poor grades and test scores, Mitchell had a couple of felonies on his record.

"I can't believe this kid is even thinking about getting an education here," said an incredulous Delaney. "There is no way we can take this guy."

"Well Regina," began Carter, "Too late. I already approved and accepted his transcript."

"What?"

"You didn't see these stats, did you? They weren't on his transcript."

"What stats?"

Carter handed Delaney a piece of paper.

"The stats that say Mitchell averaged 31 points and 14 rebounds per game in high school," said Carter. "I also got a letter from Coach Huggins."

"What did the letter say?"

"Well, I'll read it to you. 'Dear Mr. Carter: As you know a fine young man named Dewayne L. Mitchell is applying for admission to West Virginia University. I am sure he will have no problem gaining admittance. By the way Mr. Carter, you do like your job, don't you? Sincerely, Bob Huggins, Men's Basketball Coach, West Virginia University.'"

"Well Brad, it looks like we have a new power forward."

"Yep, sure looks that way."

THE CONFESSIONAL

The young boy walked apprehensively into the confessional.

"Bless me Father for I have sinned," said young Billy. "It has been like six weeks since my last confession."

The priest leaned forward. "Tell me more."

"Well, I was mad at God," Billy said. "And I said some bad words."

"Don't tell me what you said," Father Dan replied. "But why were you mad at God?"

"My daddy made me a Notre Dame fan and told me about all the National Championships Notre Dame won before I was born."

"And?"

"Well, I'm 11-years-old and I've never seen Notre Dame win a National Championship."

"Well, maybe other teams have been better."

"Yeah. Maybe. But I thought God was a Notre Dame fan. I mean Notre Dame is a Catholic school, right? He even let Boston College beat us six times in a row."

"Well Billy, Boston College is a Catholic school too."

"But my daddy said Boston College is where the bad Catholics go and Notre Dame is where the good Catholics go and that God likes Notre Dame better. So why does God let Boston College beat Notre Dame?"

"Mmm. Good question Billy. Let me tell you this, God loves all football teams. He plays no favorites. The better team wins most of the time."

"And that's why I'm mad at God. He should have Notre Dame win all the time. Who cares about Florida and

Nebraska and USC? I was taught that God was a Notre Dame fan by Sister Maria in religion class at my school. You even told me Father Dan that you were a Notre Dame fan."

"Yes, that's true." Father Dan thought for a moment in silence then said, "If we both say a few prayers for Notre Dame to win this year would that make you feel better?"

"Yes, it would."

"I'll even say a special prayer to God asking that Notre Dame have a great season."

"Like the old days?"

"Yes, like the old days."

"Thanks Father Dan."

"No, thank you Billy."

"Ok, I'm going to go now."

"Billy?"

"Yes?"

"I want twenty Hail Mary's."

"Twenty Hail Mary's?"

"You know, for the bad words. Remember?"

"Oh yes. Thank you Father Dan. Go Irish!"

"Go Irish!"

With that, young Billy exited Our Lady of Peace Church confident that a special season was in store for his beloved Fighting Irish of Notre Dame.

FAN STUDY

Long a rumor, it has now been confirmed. Fans of the New York Yankees, New York Giants, New York Rangers and Notre Dame football are superior human beings.

A comprehensive study by the William D. Jones Institute of Societal Research shows that fans of those teams are more intelligent than fans of other teams.

"Yankees, Giants, Rangers and Fighting Irish fans are not only more intelligent than the common fan, they are better looking too," said lead researcher Lars Lifrak. "We found they are more successful, compassionate and empathetic and have less psychological issues than fans of those other teams."

Assistant researcher Daniela Garrity added, "We learned that fans of the Red Sox, Mets, Cowboys, Islanders and all teams Philadelphia are basically human forms of vermin. Dumb, stupid and butt-ugly as well."

"And they have poor personal hygiene," said Lifrak. "Of course, if these people did have a brain they would be fans of the Yankees, Giants, Rangers and Notre Dame."

Radio host Bill Rogan said, "After reviewing the facts put forth by Mr. Lifrak in his exhaustive study, I would have to agree with his conclusions, one-hundred percent."

LAME VACATION

Chris Reed was excited to visit England for the first time. The Iowa native had never been out of the United States and was looking forward to seeing some Premier League soccer matches.

"Man, I'm from Iowa," Reed explained. "I need some excitement in my life."

The first game he attended was an Everton-Liverpool match up. He was ready for some action. What Chris got instead was disappointment.

"I was told these teams were fierce rivals," Reed said. "I naturally assumed there would be some entertaining hooliganism and rioting associated with the game. I was wrong. Not only were there no ugly incidents, the game was a 1-0 borefest. Oh, excuse me, 1-nil. I can't even remember who won."

Next up was a Manchester City versus Manchester United match up.

"I assumed there would be some sort of violence coming from that game. I was looking forward to some good old fashioned brawling. Nope. Nothing. Except another 1-nil result. Very disappointing."

Reed gave it one more shot. He just knew there would be a bunch of drunkards fighting, vandalizing and creating mayhem at the Tottenham-Arsenal match.

"I was certain there would be chaos and havoc related to this game," Reed said. "I couldn't believe it. It was civilized. Not only that but it turned out to be a wild 2-1 shootout. Three goals in a soccer game? Are you kidding me? Shocking. But not as shocking as coming all the way over here and not seeing one random violent act associated with soccer. I thought the English were first class hooligans. I was wrong. They are soft. Too bad the English aren't passionate about soccer. Although, come to think of it, what is there to be passionate about?"

Chris looked out the window for a moment then continued. "At least the food was good. Wait. No it wasn't. Man, this was the worst vacation ever."

BALLPARK CUISINE

"I'll have a couple of hot dogs and some nachos," said Chad Yurkovicz to Mary, the lady behind the concessions counter at Miller Park in Milwaukee. "Give me a large beer too."

A season ticket holder of the Brewers for years, Chad was usually the first fan to arrive at the game and usually the last to leave.

"I like to get here early for the bratwursts," Chad explained. "I like to get them right off the grill. Then, during batting practice, there is time to visit one of the ballpark restaurants. I tell you, there is no better dining experience than eating at the ballpark."

Chad was a popular figure among the fans who marveled at his enormous appetite.

One July day Chad had to miss a Brewers game to visit his doctor. He was having some chest pains and he couldn't figure out why.

"I'm looking at your cholesterol levels," said Doctor Michael Skelly. "And I have to ask you Chad. How do I put this? What the hell are you eating?"

Chad told to the doctor his eating regimen.

"Chad, you are four-hundred pounds. You can't be eating that stuff. Ballpark food is bad for you Chad. Very bad," said Doctor Skelly.

"Ballpark food is bad? Really?"

"Yes Chad, it's really bad."

Chad was forlorn. He was always led to believe that ballpark food was healthy fare. Apparently it wasn't.

At the next home stand, Chad walked up to the concessions counter and made his order.

"Give me a brat, a couple of hot dogs, nachos, fries and a large beer," Chad said. "What the hell do those doctors know anyway? Hey, add a cheeseburger to that Mary. Go Brewers!"

The funeral for Chad Yurkovicz will be held Thursday afternoon. He is survived by his ex-wife Madeline and Yount, his beloved bulldog. Yurkovicz was forty-one.

TROJAN TO RETURN FOR
SENIOR SEASON

Southern Cal defensive end Montrelli Ambrose, who was expected to be a high pick in the upcoming NFL draft, has announced that he is staying in school for his senior season.

A press release issued by the Trojans sports information department said that Ambrose was eager to get his degree and help the team to another BCS Bowl Game.

The release added that his admiration for head coach Lane Kiffin was another reason Ambrose was returning for his senior campaign.

When contacted at his 8,700 foot mansion in Beverly Hills, Ambrose was more forthcoming.

"Why am I coming back for my senior year? Well, many reasons. First of all I like Los Angeles. I could get drafted by Green Bay or Tennessee. God forbid Buffalo took me. Plus, the lease on my Testarossa is good for another year. But first and foremost, I'm not anxious to take a pay cut at this time."

DRAFT EXPERT EXTRAORDINAIRE

Mel Kiper Junior, NFL Draft Expert, had Kansas State offensive tackle Jon Chelesnik listed 427th on his draft board.

Kiper noted that Chelesnik, who had a nice senior season, was a project and might be a good free-agent signing.

That said, Kiper, knowing the Raiders draft history, made a bold prediction before Oakland's first round pick was announced.

"The Raiders are clueless," said the well-coiffed Kiper. "Look at some of their recent number one picks. I'm sure they'll blow it again. They need an offensive tackle. They are looking to dazzle everyone by taking a guy nobody has heard of. Al Davis heard that Chelesnik is a distant cousin of Fred Biletnikoff. Everything points to Davis and the Raiders taking Chelesnik."

Commissioner Roger Goodell strode to the podium. "With the fifth selection in the NFL Draft, the Oakland Raiders select Jon Chelesnik, offensive tackle, Kansas State. The Redskins are on the clock."

The draftniks at Radio City Music Hall in New York went wild, stunned that not only did the Raiders take Chelesnik, but that Kiper called it.

Kiper sat beaming at the ESPN Draft desk. His colleagues were amazed. It was the greatest call in NFL Draft history. Yes, Mel Kiper Junior lived up to his billing as NFL Draft Expert.

It would be a mere 364 days until Kiper, once again, became relevant.

THE HOLDOUT

Jake Perkins hit a career best .235 for the Mariners. He also set career marks in home runs (4) and RBI's (21). The third year utility infielder headed into the off-season confident he would get a huge raise.

Perkins and his wife Samantha threw some numbers around and figured a contract offer of about six-million dollars, over three years, would likely be coming their way.

Perkins agent, David Itchkawitz, said that they wouldn't settle for less than two-million per year.

It was certainly an exciting time for Jake and Samantha. They recalled the years of struggling to make ends meet in the minors. The unnerving quest of Jake trying to become an established major leaguer. All the hard work was about to pay off in a big way.

In December, Perkins hurriedly visited his mailbox, waiting for Seattle's contract offer. Every day he would venture out to get the mail and finally, the envelope he was waiting for, with Mariners letterhead, arrived.

Jake ran into the house and called for Samantha. "It's here, my contract offer." Jake opened the envelope. When he saw the figure offered by the Mariners he was crushed. It was for one year and a paltry $450,000. The league minimum was $400,000. With his production and three seasons in the big leagues the Mariners determined Jake was worth just $50,000 more than the minimum salary.

There was no other choice for Perkins. He had to hold out. Jake didn't go to spring training, but he worked out with his old high school team and went to the batting cages faithfully.

Come late March he hadn't heard from the Mariners. The standoff was getting ugly.

The season started in early April and Jake was still holding out. He only wanted a fair deal and he wasn't going to budge.

Finally, in late May one of the parties cracked. It wasn't Seattle. Jake swallowed his pride and called Mariners General Manager Jack Zduriencik.

"Hi Jack, this is Jake. I'm ready to end my hold out."

"Who?"

"Jake. Jake Perkins."

"Oh yeah, Jake. How ya doing? Hey, we thought you retired when you didn't show up for spring training. We had no idea you were holding out. Bad career move there Jake. Anyway, we have a utility infielder already so, well, take care Jake."

Jake was crushed. His baseball career looked to be over. He didn't think Home Depot would pay him the $450,000 that he could have been earning.

Samantha was already on the phone with her lawyer, hoping to divorce her greedy-ass husband.

WHAT THE?

First Lady Michelle Obama was miffed when the White House dining staff served the family dinner on paper plates with plastic utensils and Styrofoam cups.

"We're sorry Mrs. Obama," said one of the staff members. "It seems the fine china and silverware has turned up missing."

The Obama's ate their dinner wondering how such a thing could happen.

Following dinner, President Obama headed to the family room to catch some hoops on TV. He immediately noticed his big screen TV was missing.

"That's strange," thought the President. "Maybe they took it for repairs or something."

He decided to head to the Oval Office to catch up on some paperwork.

He discovered his chair was missing, as were the official White House pens and stationary. Even his favorite paperweight was gone.

As he strolled back to his family, President Obama noticed a couple of hallway paintings were missing.

Mrs. Obama greeted her husband and said, "I'm missing some things from the kitchen and bedroom. Does the staff take things to fix up or replace without telling us?"

A staffer told the Obama's that they never take anything or they would get fired. If something was broken or in need of replacement they could see that it was taken care of.

It was strange to have items missing, but the Obama's figured they must have just misplaced them or something. Not a big deal.

At bedtime, Michelle turned to her husband and asked about his day.

"It was a nice day," said the President. "I didn't have to deal with that bitch Hillary for a change. Also, it was fun having Urban Meyer and the Florida Gators tour the White House and celebrate their National Championship. Nice kids those Gators, nice kids."

THE ENTOURAGE

Cleotis McFarland was one of the up and coming stars in the NBA. He made his first All-Star game appearance in just his third season and he had all the trappings of wealth and fame.

McFarland lived in a mammoth white house with a huge heated pool and a spectacular garage that housed several cars. He kept it real by keeping his home boys on his personal staff.

The phone call from his agent, Jeff Levinson, took McFarland by surprise.

"Cleotis, this isn't going to be a pleasant conversation," Levinson began. "You've made, in basketball salary and endorsements, about twenty-four million dollars. That's the good news. The bad news is, you have about seven-thousand dollars left in your savings and checking accounts."

McFarland was stunned. He worked hard for his money and was a solid citizen. He wondered what the heck happened to his money.

Cleotis stood in his kitchen and looked into the vast living room. There he saw his old high school buddies. There was Demetrious playing a video game. The Squirrel was on his cell phone. Jeremiah was watching television. Jermaine was sleeping on the sofa. Dexter was in the bathroom and the familiar smell of marijuana was making its way into the hallway. In the backyard, Peanut was lounging by the pool and Roscoe was admiring his new gun.

It was then that McFarland knew he had to cut payroll. The entourage would have to be trimmed. It wasn't going to be easy but it had to be done; however, Cleotis thought it would be a good idea to first take away Roscoe's piece before the budgetary cuts were revealed.

A NOVEL CONCEPT

"BALL," bellowed the umpire.

The batter trotted to first base. The bases were loaded on three consecutive walks by right-hander Todd Van Horn.

Van Horn couldn't spot his fastball. He was bouncing his curve and he was wide with his slider. He didn't have confidence he could get his splitter over and the cutter wasn't cutting. None of the hitters were chasing his knuckleball and his change was constantly up in the zone.

Manager Rich Spear called time and went to visit his struggling hurler.

"What's the problem?" asked Spear.

"I just can't get any of my pitches over," said Van Horn. "I've tried them all and nothing is working."

"I have a new pitch you can throw."

"What's that?"

"It's called a strike."

With that, the exasperated manager turned away and headed back to the dugout.

COMMISSIONER CALLS
IT QUITS

Clem Ferris, the commissioner of the Denver 70+ Division of the National Adult Baseball Association, has told the Denver Post that he has decided to retire.

"I started playing in the 70+ league sixteen years ago and became commissioner ten years ago," said Ferris, 86. "The time has come to step down."

Ferris recounts a couple of stories from his treasure trove of memories.

"Ah, where to begin," said Ferris. "There was the bench clearing brawl in 2002 between the Windbags and Codgers. There were a few broken hips in that one. Had to suspend several guys for that."

Numerous players made a lasting impression on Ferris.

"I remember Harry Luttenberg of the Geezers pulling his groin walking from the dugout to the mound before the start of the championship game a few years back. Hadn't seen that before. Speaking of pitchers, we had to suspend Jim O'Connor for throwing a spitball. However, I rescinded that suspension when I was presented with visual evidence that he was inadvertently drooling on the ball and was not intentionally loading it up."

Clem was surrounded by baseball memorabilia in his office as he continued to share his memories.

"We had one guy, Caspar Fishbein, who had Alzheimer's," recalled Ferris. "He hit a grounder one day and ran to third base. Another time, he caught a pop up and then ran and slid into second base. The last I saw him was when he was playing center field one moment and the next minute he was gone. He apparently wandered off and that was the end of his career. Baseball is known for players exhibiting flaky behavior and Caspar was the flakiest of them all."

While it was fun being commissioner, nothing beat playing the game for Ferris.

"I loved to play. I gave it up three years ago when I kept tripping over my colostomy bag. That was embarrassing, but not as embarrassing as when my dentures fell out when I was arguing with the umpire one day. I got thrown out of the game for that one."

Ferris is officially out of the game that he has loved and participated in since he was a youngster. One wonders what will his plans be?

"I'm moving in with my son and his yappy wife in Bradenton. Yep, heading to Florida to rot away like the rest of us washed up ballplayers. Damn."

THE ELEVATOR RIDE

Dennis, a football fanatic, initiated some small talk in the elevator.

"So, you did you watch the Broncos yesterday?"

"Of course," was the reply from the other lone passenger. "I was very pleased with the running game. The offensive line was really opening some holes. Royal made some nice catches too. I think he'll end up in the Pro Bowl. The defensive line also had a good game for a change. I noticed they were stunting more than usual and because they were getting pressure on the quarterback they didn't have to blitz as much. It's still spotty on the special teams, but its still early in the season. I've been encouraged by some of the rookies, but there is still a learning curve. Wouldn't you agree?"

Dennis was distracted, but still managed to answer, "Yeah, I'd most definitely agree."

The chatty passenger continued. "Overall, I'd grade it a B-plus effort. The Chiefs aren't very good and we should have beaten them by more than 13 points. The killer instinct is something we need to develop. We let them stay in the game too long. So, who do you like in tonight's Vikings-Packers game?"

Dennis hesitated and then said, "Uh, the Packers."

While Margaret wasn't much to look at Dennis realized something right away. He was in love. It was a most fortunate elevator ride for both of them.

PLENTY O' MUD AND JELLO

It had been decades since Salt Lake City had a sporting event of this magnitude and caliber. It was long over-due.

A line of anxious wrestling fans extended, three deep, all the way around the block. Electricity filled the air.

The building's bright red lights shone down on the fans waiting to get into the event. The excitement felt, by the predominantly male crowd, was off the charts.

The marquee said it all—Soccer Moms vs Hockey Moms. Tonight Only!

TRADING PLACES?

During a time out, John Castellano took a close look at the Broncos milling about on the sidelines. The game was well in hand with the Broncos putting the finishing touches on a 35-10 win over the Chargers.

Castellano, a successful businessman and long-time season ticket holder, pondered what it must be like to be an NFL player, especially with the Broncos. He thought of the fame, the fortune and the exhilarating feeling of winning a big game like today.

"Man, what a life those guys lead. They don't know how lucky they are," he thought.

At that exact moment, Broncos offensive lineman Chad Lucero took a drink from a water bottle. His left arm was numb. His right ankle was sprained and he had a headache that was unbearable. He had bruised ribs and his hamstrings were tight. Lucero wondered how he would sleep that evening.

As he looked into the crowd he thought, "Man, those guys have it made. They come watch us play on Sunday, work an easy job during the week and get to spend quality time with their families. I got my head buried in a playbook while I sit in a tub of ice all week scarfing down anti-inflammatories."

THE TRAVELER

Of course the airline lost his luggage. It always seemed to happen at this particular airport.

"Oh well," thought the traveler.

The gentleman calmly voiced his complaint to an unconcerned baggage handling agent and then sought a cab.

After several empty cabs refused to pick him up, he finally got hold of a taxi to bring him to his downtown hotel.

"That'll be $140," said the cabbie.

"$140? Are you serious," asked the athletic looking passenger. "What a rip-off."

After dutifully paying, he entered the hotel. It didn't make him feel better when the guy in front of him didn't hold open the heavy door and it slammed into him.

"We don't have your room ready," the front desk clerk curtly said. "You'll have to wait."

The trip certainly wasn't getting off to a good start.

After finally getting his key, the visitor arrived in his room. It was supposed to be a suite, but he was tired and didn't feel like dealing with the inhospitable staff on the phone. He certainly wasn't going back down to the lobby to complain.

He picked up the phone and ordered room service. Two hours later his meal still hadn't arrived despite promises that it would be there in five minutes, after each inquisitive call.

After washing his hands, he realized he didn't have any towels. He called the front desk.

"Hi, I'm in room 2241. I need some towels please."

"We'll see," was the discourteous reply. "We're

pretty busy here and you aren't the only guest here ya' know."

Finally, the man decided to go out to a restaurant. The steakhouse initially messed up his order and when the correct meal came, the meat was overcooked and the mashed potatoes were lumpy. Even the bread was stale and his drink warm.

"Not my problem," the Maitre'D said.

Not one to complain, the patron left a nice tip and went for a walk.

An older woman walked right into him and then had the nerve to say, "Watch where you're going idiot."

"That was rude," the irritated traveler thought.

A few minutes later, as he was waiting to cross the street, a man let his dog urinate on his pants leg.

"Hey, what are you doing," he said. "Get that dog away from me."

"Shut your face," said the burly dog owner.

After returning to the hotel and waiting for the elevator the out-of-towner politely said to a bellhop, "Hi, how's it going?"

"What do you care?" was the nasty reply.

Of course, to top off the day, the elevator got stuck on the 15th floor. It was no wonder that John Elway always hated making business trips to Cleveland.

KENNY'S FUTURE

Kenny lacked ambition and motivation. His grades were dismal at best. His college entrance test scores were horrid. Basically, Kenny was a slacker who was on track to barely graduate from Stevenson High in Illinois.

"Unfortunately, we have to graduate Kenny," said academic advisor Will Bartholomew. "I mean, we can't keep him here forever and by the time he is truly ready to graduate he'll be in his thirties. Look, he's a nice kid, but dumber than a box of rocks."

The day came when Kenny had to meet with Bartholomew to discuss his future. It was a meeting neither looked forward to.

"So, Kenny, what do you want to do with the rest of your life?" asked Bartholomew.

"I don't know," was Kenny's reply as he shrugged his shoulders.

"Well, what do you like?"

"Nothing really."

"Come on Kenny, you have to like something."

"I like sports I guess. That's kind of fun."

"What else do you like Kenny?"

"Mmmm. Uh, I like listening to the radio."

Will leaned back in his chair and thought for a few minutes.

"Have you ever thought of working in sports radio Kenny?"

"You mean like a sports announcer?"

"No, I don't think you have what it takes to actually broadcast sports. That takes actual skill, talent and intelligence; however, you really have what it takes to be in management."

"Management?"

"Absolutely Kenny. You are highly qualified to be a program director or general manager of a radio station."

"Me? Really?"

"Absolutely. You don't need to know anything for that. It's easy and all you have to do is blame other people for any problems that arise and take credit when things go well. Cake."

"Well, it sounds interesting. OK, I'm in."

A few short weeks later, Kenny was enrolled in the Michael J. Carsella School of Broadcasting and well on his way to becoming a program director or general manager of a real live radio station.

THE TRANSLATOR

"Welcome back to the post-game show. I'm Kevin Burkhart and our player of the game is Mets right-hander Pablo Sanchez, who not only tossed a complete game shutout in the Mets 5-0 win over the Cubs, but also knocked in a couple of runs with his first career homer.

"With us is translator Roberto Nunez. Roberto, ask Pablo, how did he feel out there today?"

"Pablo, como te sentiste en el juego hoy?"

"Me senti muy bien en el campo hoy."

"Pablo says that he felt very good out there today and that he felt strong the entire game and that he really was glad to contribute to the win and he feels that with the proper work between starts that he'll be able to duplicate his performance today, God willing."

"Roberto, ask Pablo what was his key to success?"

"Ok. Pablo, cual fue la llave a el exito?"

"Um, era importante de adelantarsele a los bateadores y afortunadamente lo pude lograr. Use la bola rapida para acomodar a los bateadores y la bola en curva para acabar con ellos. Tambien tengo que darle credito a el catcher que marco muy bien, la defense hizo un buen trabajo, y bueno en si el esfuerzo es de todo el equipo."

"Pablo says that he got ahead of the hitters and he had good control."

"Our guest is winning pitcher Pablo Sanchez. Helping us is translator Roberto Nunez. Roberto, ask Pablo, how big a win was this for the Mets?"

"Que tan importante fue ganar este juego?"

"Si, fue una victoria grande. Realmente la necesitabamos para regresar a la lucha," replied Pablo.

"Pablo said that it was a huge win for the team. We've been struggling and can't afford to lose any ground to the first place team the Phillies. He also said that the attitude of the team has been very good during the losing streak, but today's win gives the team confidence they can go on a hot streak and that he was just happy to contribute to such an important win."

"Ask Pablo, Roberto, what was your approach?"

"Sure. Pablo, cual fue tu enfoque?"

"Mi enfoque fue de ser agresivo. Necesitaba con centrarme en el juego. A veces suelo a perder el enfoque asi que tuve que ser intenso. Revise los reportes, tuve una Buena preparacion en el bullpen y puse toda mi confianza en el catcher y mi entrenador. Realmente valio la pena todo. El beisbol es un jeugo de ajustes y hoy fui e apaz de mejorar mientras el juego avanzo."

"Pablo says his approach was to be aggressive."

"Pablo congrats on the win and thanks for your time and Roberto thanks for translating."

"You're welcome Kevin."

"De nada."

"That's the story from the Mets clubhouse, now let's send it back upstairs to Gary and Keith."

TOM THE MISGUIDED

Tom Morello grew up in Niles, Michigan; a small, sleepy town not far from the Indiana border. As a kid, he would go to nearby South Bend, Indiana to sell programs at Notre Dame football games. So, naturally, it was assumed that Tom was a Notre Dame fan.

The assumption bothered the hyperactive football fan. "I'm not a Notre Dame fan, never have been a Notre Dame fan and never will be a Notre Dame fan."

As a young man, Tom watched a Notre Dame-Michigan State game at a friend's house.

"I hope the Spartans win," said Tom. "To hell with Notre Dame!"

Tom was kicked out of the house.

Soon after, Tom enrolled at Michigan State and went about his life, rooting for the Spartans and rooting against Notre Dame.

The years went by and Tom raised a family of Michigan State fans and Notre Dame haters. Despite being shunned by many for his football beliefs, he held to his misguided convictions.

Eventually, the day came when Tom met his maker. He went out quietly with his family at his beside.

The elderly spiritual man had lived a good life and was on his way to heaven.

At the Pearly Gates, Tom received a scare from Saint Peter. "Hello Tom, we've been waiting for you."

"Hi Saint Peter. I've heard a lot about you. I'm ready to enter Heaven."

"Well, not so fast Tom."

"What do you mean?"

"Remember the day you were at your friend Bill's house?"

"No."

"You remember Tom. The Michigan State game when you said, 'To hell with Notre Dame.' Do you remember now?"

"I never said that."

"Are you sure about that Tom?"

"Well, I don't think I said that."

"Let's take a look at the monitor Tom."

Tom and Saint Peter walked over to the big screen television. Saint Peter pressed a couple of buttons and sure enough, there was Tom, as a young man, uttering the words, "To hell with Notre Dame!"

"Would you like me to replay that Tom?" asked Saint Peter.

"No. I'm sorry. I mean, uh, I didn't mean it that way."

"That was a serious transgression Tom, very serious. I don't know if we can allow you to enter."

"Oh no!" said a visibly shaken Tom. "Please! I was good most of my life, I really was."

"I know," chuckled Saint Peter, "I'm just messing with you! Hey, just get in line over there and it will be a few moments before you'll be in heaven."

"Thanks Saint Peter," said an extremely relieved Tom Morello.

Once in Heaven, Tom looked around. He noticed a bunch of people sitting around a television screen. They were watching a football game. A Notre Dame football game.

After a few minutes of watching, Tom mustered the nerve to say, "Hey, does anyone know where I can watch the Michigan State game? We're playing Purdue today."

The people watching the game turned and looked at Tom.

"Who are you?" asked one of the men.

"I'm Tom the new guy. Tom Morello, Niles, Michigan."

"Look Tom, we don't know how you got in here, but there is something you should know. We only watch Notre Dame football games up here. Notre Dame hoops too."

"What about watching Michigan State?"

"We watch Michigan State too," said another man. "Once a year when they play Notre Dame!"

The rest of the people laughed loudly.

"But I want to watch Michigan State," said a despondent Tom.

A man piped up to help Tom.

"Well sir, there is a place where you can go watch Michigan State and all the other Big 10 teams, but it's not here."

"Thanks," said Tom.

A week later, Tom was watching Michigan State take on Michigan with all the other Spartan and Wolverine fans. It was awfully hot from where they were watching. Awfully hot.

HOW GEHRIG'S STREAK REALLY STARTED

Broadcasting legend Paul Harvey passed away on February 28th, 2009. Here was a story that he was prepared to read for his March 1st newscast but never did. ...

In the sport light, Wally Pipp was a fine first baseman for the Yankees in the early to mid 1920's. He was a slick fielder and good RBI man. He also routinely hit over .300. Of course, the story went that Wally had a headache one day and let the kid, Lou Gehrig, play. But the real reason why Pipp left the lineup was because he had received death threats.

Sealed documents were recently opened and showed that Pipp was the apparent target of a hitman; a gambler perhaps. Nobody knows, but somebody wanted Pipp out of the Yankees lineup. The last death threat was sent to Manager Miller Huggins. It was on old paper with cut out lettering, from newspapers. It stated that Pipp would be killed if he was in the lineup on June 2, 1925.

Huggins felt he had no choice but to bench Pipp and put in the new kid from Columbia University—Lou Gehrig. The team concocted a story that Pipp had a headache and would take a seat on the bench.

Well, Gehrig did replace Pipp for a day and more. Gehrig took over first base and didn't leave the lineup for 2,130 games. A rather costly headache for Pipp who would be traded to Cincinnati after the season. And so the story goes.

But there's more. Modern day DNA testing has discovered that the person who sent those letters was none other than Gehrig himself. Now you know the rest of the story. I'm Paul Harvey. Good Day!

TALKIN' SPORTS

"My bowling average was 322."

"For a series?"

"No, per game."

"John Elway should have stuck with hockey."

"Yeah, he was a horrible linebacker."

"Do you think the Avs will win the NBA championship?"

"Not unless Helton is playing for them."

"Jamey Carroll was the best player ever for the Avalanche."

"Yeah, he should be in the Hall of Fame."

"So should Casey Bloyer."

"Is he the Broncos quarterback?"

"Yeah. And some radio guy."

"I'm hungry. I could eat a sneaker."

"I once ran a three minute mile."

"Really?"

"Yeah."

"Hey fellas, I heard about that."

"Cool."

"I once won a million dollar bet."

"On what?"

"That the Lions would win the Super Bowl."

"The Lions won the Super Bowl?"

"Yeah, like five years ago. Won a million bucks."

"Does anyone want to buy some Carmelo Anthony autographs? I just signed some pictures."

"I would have to say the Steelers and Twins is the best rivalry in sports."

"Better than Iowa State and the Lakers?"

"I think that the San Francisco Giants and Pensacola High is a better rivalry."

"Do they play each other?"

"Yeah, in spring training."

"Did you see Obama wearing a White Sox jacket at the All Star game?"

"And he hit a double during the game."

"Yeah, I saw that."

"Not bad. I heard he was like some big shot in politics."

"He's the mayor of Chicago or something like that when he's not playing for the White Sox."

"Do you think they'll let us go to the winter Olympics in Mexico next year?"

"Damn, here comes the nurse."

"Ok guys, time to get ready for bed," said nurse Nan Hughes. "Lights out in ten minutes."

Yes, just another night talking sports at the Clifford L. Powers Institute for Diminished Cranial Capacity.

TORTURE BY SPORTS TALK

Alleged torture tactics used by US Military officials at Guantanamo Bay have come under scrutiny by the international community.

Unsubstantiated reports indicate that American sports talk radio programming has been played nonstop in the prison cells of suspected terrorists. The constant airing of Jim Rome, Chris "Mad Dog" Russo, Steve Czaban and others has caused concern among several human rights groups.

Clive Duncan with Amnesty International said, "If these accusations are true, then there is no excuse for this type of criminal behavior. Having to listen to sports talk radio is not only unbearable, but inhumane."

One prisoner, Akim Bakim Hakim said, "The filthy American's torture us with unbearable sports talk. It is driving us crazy. We demand water boarding back. That was better than listening to Andy Cornell or Sandy Clough."

"Aw, the poor little terrorists can't listen to American sports talk," US General William Thornton responded. "Well, I can't blame them. I can't listen to that crap either. But hey, I'm not a terrorist and I can make the choice not to listen. Still, it is pretty harsh interrogation now that you mention it, but that's the point you jackass."

Several prisoners have cracked and ratted out suspected terrorists or terroristic plots. Others have done even better by committing suicide.

United States President Barack Obama has denounced the torture-by-sports-talk-show-host method of interrogation.

"This is disgraceful. As a foreign nationalist ...I mean as a concerned American, I denounce these torturous methods. I hereby decree that we set all of the prisoners free."

TAPING MILESTONE

Packers running back Ryan Grant looked at the tape job and said, "Feels good, thanks Doc."

As soon as Grant hopped off the table the celebration began.

Sirens blared, streamers and confetti flew and the entire team entered the training area, at least as many that could be crammed into the small room.

Now in his thirty-ninth year as an assistant trainer for the Packers, Percy "Doc" Patterson had just taped his 500,000th ankle.

"I'm overwhelmed," said Patterson. "I just chalk it up to a lot of ankles that needed to be taped and the fact I could never find a better job. I mean it sounds glamorous, but have you seen what the ankles and feet of NFL players look and smell like? I've seen more toe fungus than any human alive."

Packers Head Trainer Pepper Burruss, no relation to Plaxico, said, "Doc is the best ankle taper guy I've ever seen. John Norwig of the Steelers is pretty good they say, but no way can he measure up to Doc."

While Patterson is the gold standard of ankle tapers it wasn't always that way. He remembers his career was almost over before it started.

"My very first professional ankle tape job was for Bart Starr," recalled Patterson. "Bart was reading his playbook when I accidentally started the taping too high up the leg and pulled off some hair. He yelled in pain. I would have thought a two-time Super Bowl MVP would have a higher pain threshold. Anyway, Bart shot me a glare and I thought I was done. But when he got on the field he remarked how good his ankles felt, especially his bothersome right ankle. Or was it his left? Wait, it was his right. Although maybe it was his left. Yeah, it was his left ankle. Actually, now that I think about it, it was his right ankle. I think. Anyway, Bart's validation of my taping skills has led me to this career and living in freezing cold Green Bay all these years, maxing out at $12.50 an hour. I'm grateful to Bart, sort-of."

Commissioner Roger Goodell sent a congratulatory telegram and a $100 voucher to the NFL's online gift shop. "I'm really sorry that a previous commitment prevented me from making it to Green Bay and witnessing athletic training history. We'll certainly honor Doc Patterson next summer at halftime of the Hall of Fame game in Canton."

When asked what his previous commitment was, the commissioner answered, "There was no previous commitment, but if you think I'm going all the way to Green Bay to celebrate some guy taping ankles then you're crazy. Just keep that off the record please."

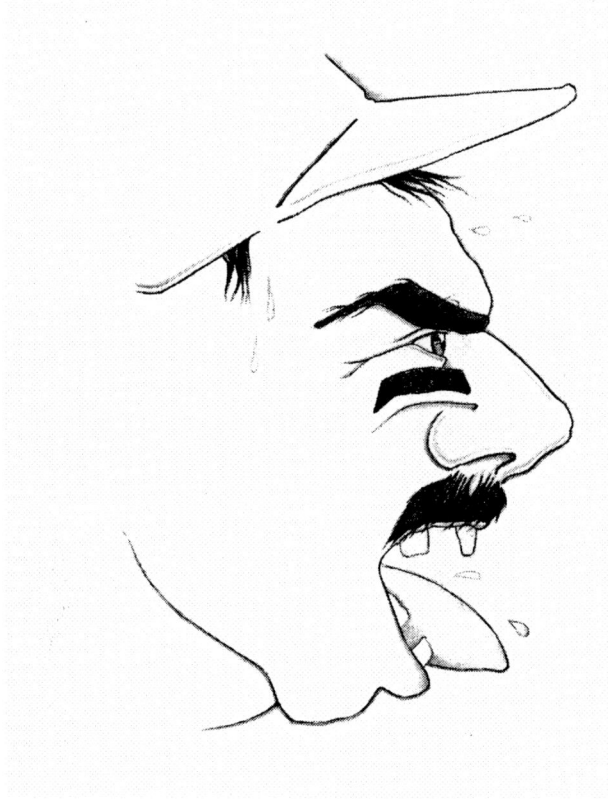

THE GAMER

The pitch came in tantalizingly slow. To Troy Fickler, it appeared outside so he let it go by.

"Steeeeerike three!" was the umpire's call.

Three outs and the bases left loaded.

Troy was not happy.

He tossed his bat and got in the umpire's face. Then he peeled off his batting gloves and threw them at the umpire's feet.

"You are a dead man. You hear me? A dead man," yelled Troy inches from the ump's face. "That was a $%#(^$@#* rotten call. I'll see you in the parking lot after the game!"

His teammates tried to intervene, but the furious Fickler continued his tirade. He kicked dirt on home plate. He shoved his own teammates. He was swearing up a storm that only got worse when the patient umpire tossed him from the game.

When he finally returned to the bench, he threw bats and balls onto the field. He turned over a garbage can. When his wife came over to quiet Fickler, he yelled and cursed at her too.

A true competitor, anyone can understand Fickler's anger and frustration. After all, it was a key point in the game and Fickler's team ended up losing 11-10 to drop to 4-7 in the Aurora Men's Slow Pitch Twilight Softball League.

THE BLAME GAME

Don't dare bring up the name Gottfried Schmidt around Fred Skolarzik.

"That Schmidt guy ruined my life," said Skolarzik. "He ruined a lot of lives. I'm glad he's dead."

Skolarzik was a human pinsetter at Strike Out Lanes, a once popular bowling alley in Milwaukee in the late forties and early fifties.

"I was a pinsetter starting when I was 11-years-old," recalled Skolarzik, now 77. "My dad was a pinsetter and my grandfather was a pinsetter. It was the family business and I was looking forward to a long, rewarding career setting pins. And it was all taken away from me."

As a teen, Skolarzik and the other pinsetters heard rumors of a machine that would be able to set pins automatically.

"That sounded like a pipe dream," Skolarzik said. "I mean, how could a machine do what we did? Impossible, or so I thought. Schmidt. That damn Schmidt."

In 1946, Gottfried Schmidt invented the automatic pinsetter. By the mid-fifties bowling alleys worldwide began replacing human pinsetters with the new machines. The automatic pinsetters changed the course of bowling history and put thousands of human pinsetters out of work.

Cletus Benhower, 73, was a pinsetter who worked with Skolarzik in the fifties. "I remember the day in 1954 when the bowling alley shut down for a week to install the new pin setting and ball retrieval machines. I was actually kind of glad. I was tired of setting pins all day and night. It was loud, hot and boring, but Fred loved it. When he was told his services were no longer needed he went off the deep end. I heard he became bitter and never recovered. Me? I went to college and just retired after a law career."

Skolarzik feels his life would have been different if not for Schmidt. "He basically took away my livelihood when I was 22. He cost thousands of people their jobs and ruined their lives. He ruined my life and I will never forgive him."

Meanwhile, David Schmidt, 27, of Santa Barbara, California, the grandson of Gottfried Schmidt, when told of Skolarzik's story said, "He says my grandpa ruined his life and the lives of others with his invention? Wow, that's interesting. I almost feel guilty now inheriting the 35-million dollars my grandpa left behind for me. Yep, I almost feel guilty, but I don't."

HOW ABOUT THE
ALIVE PART?

Johnnie Lee Kincaid saw an opening and went for it. He accelerated through the turn, but clipped the bumper of Rusty Wallace and went into a spin. Kincaid's car then hit the wall, rolled over several times, was hit by another car and came to a spinning halt on the infield grass. The car was shredded apart and what was left was engulfed by flames.

Somehow, Kincaid crawled out of the wreckage and within seconds a crew was dousing the flames on his jumpsuit.

Veteran NASCAR observers said it was the most frightening crash they had seen in a long, long time. They were amazed that Kincaid escaped with just a bruised left wrist.

"I'm not only disappointed, but I'm angry," said Kincaid. "What a complete waste of time today was. This will put me back in the standings and with my wrist I don't know if I'll be able to race at Talladega next week for my wonderful sponsors, 7-Up, Ivory Soap, Dish Network, The Men's Warehouse, Nokia, Pizza Hut, Lucien Piccard Watches, The Outback Steakhouse, Sunoco, Valvoline, Adidas ..."

ALL ABOUT THE KIDS

Commissioner David Stern is proud to host the first "NBA Illegitimate Kids Convention" this Saturday afternoon at Madison Square Garden in New York.

"Originally we planned to hold this in the Marriot Hotel Ballroom," said Stern. "However, we vastly underestimated the number of little bastards produced by our players, so we moved it to the Garden."

The event will provide an outlet for illegitimate children to vent about their miserable lives due to the fact that their absentee dads won't fork over child support payments and mom is only interested in sleeping with the next NBA player she can find. Counselors will be on hand to lend support to the whiny kids and attorneys will be in attendance trying to shake down support payments from the deadbeat dads.

"My dad isn't part of my life," said DeJuan Jenkins, 26, son of former Pacers Forward Lionel Lincoln. "Because he didn't give us child support and because my mom was too busy sleeping around with any pro athlete she could find, my life is a mess. I dropped out of school. I can't keep a job and I'm a crack addict. I wish I was never born and that would have been the case if I had responsible parents."

Former Bulls forward Mason Daffey, who has ten illegitimate kids from eight different mamas, was expected to be the keynote speaker but cancelled.

"I wanted to meet my kids at the convention," said Daffey. "But when I heard lawyers would be there, no way. I'm not gonna fall for that trick. I've been duped plenty of times before. Well, at least ten times."

Many are praising the Illegitimate Kids Convention as a way to influence dad-less children in a positive way including NFL Commissioner Roger Goodell.

"I think this is something that we would like to emulate. Although, with our league I think we'll have to rent out the Los Angeles Coliseum or Rhode Island for our Kids Convention."

INDISCRETION

Flashbulbs were going off as embattled Reverend Gregory Carr stood at the podium. Hundreds of reporters were anxious to grill the once wildly popular Reverend.

"What can I say," said embattled Carr. "I should have never put myself in that situation. It is what it is and I'm sorry."

Reverend Carr told some friends that he was going from his Annapolis home to Baltimore to attend an afternoon social at a VFW hall. Instead, Carr gave into temptation and traveled to Camden Yards to take in an Orioles game.

With his wife Peggy by his side, and after weeks of denials, Carr finally admitted, "Yes, I went to see the Orioles play. I'm sorry I've let so many people down."

Carr further explained how he would park his car in Glen Burnie and take a cab to the ballpark. On many occasions he went to O's games in disguise including once as the Orioles unpopular bird mascot.

He would schedule business trips around Orioles road games because he felt it would be easier to hide his allegiance in other ballparks. If anyone talked about the Orioles, he would change the subject.

Carr admitted to being an Orioles fan dating back to the Brooks Robinson days.

"Back then it was cool to be an O's fan," said Carr. "But now? Man, it's tough. And because of my loyalty to the O's I'm a laughingstock. I knew I shouldn't have gone to the game." He shook his head. "I hope to emerge from this embarrassing episode stronger than ever."

His son Mike stated, "We are standing behind dad.

We are, of course, shocked. This is a side of him we didn't know about. The sad thing is, all this could have been averted had he been a Yankees fan."

MEMORIES

The home run. That's all everyone wanted to talk to Rick Schultz about; the game winning little league home run he hit for the Poughkeepsie Cubs.

"The home run?" chuckled Rick. "Well alright, the home run. So we were trailing all game long. If memory serves correctly, we were down 5-3 in the last inning with two outs. If we win we go to the playoffs. If we lose the season is over."

The elderly gentleman leaned closer and said, "So what happened?"

"Well, Alec Calhoun got a single up the middle, then Carl Garafalo stepped up to the plate. Carl was usually an automatic out but this time we caught a break when Carl got hit in the head with a pitch. I think Kevin Gleason ran for him. Anyway, it was up to me, the smallest guy on the team. The count was 2-1. Wait, I think it was 2-2. The Red Sox pitcher threw me a fastball and I connected and sent it over the left field fence for a game winning three-run homer. All my teammates mobbed me when I got home. It was the biggest moment of my athletic career. Never experienced anything like it since. Still, it was a great thrill and the highlight of my baseball career. I'll never forget it. Gosh, time really flies, doesn't it? Man, it seems like only yesterday that I hit that homer. Well, gotta go Grandpa."

With that, 11-year-old Rickey Schultz hopped on his bike to join his friends at the pool and to probably relive memories of the game winning three run homer he belted—yesterday.

A CONTENTIOUS
RELATIONSHIP

Gary Pratzer was strolling through New York's Central Park when he spotted an attractive young lady sitting on a bench.

She was reading a book and enjoying the warm summer afternoon. Beside her was a violin case.

Gary walked up to the woman and introduced himself.

"Hi, my name is Gary and I noticed you have a violin with you. Where do you play?"

"I'm Amanda," the woman said. "I'm with the New York Philharmonic. I joined them just after college."

"Really? Wow, you must be good," Gary replied. "I'm also into music. I play the tuba."

Amanda looked at him with a little more interest.

"Nice. Where do you play?" she asked.

"Well, I don't play professionally," he said. "I used to play in The Ohio State Marching Band. You may have seen me dot the I on TV at the horseshoe my senior year against Michigan."

"Yeah, I probably saw it. Have a nice day," Amanda said coldly.

"Is something wrong?" asked Gary.

"Yeah, you," Amanda answered. "I was in the Michigan band and I don't wish to speak to a Buckeye who was part of the lamest tradition in college football. Dotting the I? Come on, that's weak."

"Well, when Michigan beats Ohio State maybe you can talk. I think whipping your asses every year is a pretty good tradition. Oh yeah, even Purdue's band is better than your sorry band."

"You play the tuba. Shut up."

"Oh, the violin is soooo hard. I bet mommy and daddy sprung for lessons when you were six."

"I was five. And they sent me to a good school too. Not that dump in Columbus. Hey, how's Maurice Clarett doing these days."

"How does 3-9 sound or does the band even know how bad your team was last season?"

Little did the pair realize that this was just the beginning of a beautiful relationship—kinda.

A TURF GOLF OUTING

Casey Bloyer was tormented by the fact that he had never scored a hole-in-one. It especially hurt because his dad and his brother had made hole-in-ones. Just about everybody who Casey knew experienced that glorious moment when the ball plunked into the hole from the tee box.

Sure he had come close a few times. One time at Green Valley Ranch in Denver his tee shot was rolling directly towards the hole. Two feet from the cup, out of nowhere, a golden retriever ran onto the green, grabbed the ball in its mouth and took off.

Once, while playing at the Riviera Country Club in California, Casey's tee shot was heading right towards the hole. It had a chance, but a sudden minor earthquake hit and the slight tremor steered the ball inches wide of the cup.

"I don't think I could ever hit a ball more perfectly," said Bloyer. "When the earthquake hit I figured somebody doesn't want me to get a hole-in-one."

That brings us to a recent outing at the Wellshire Golf Club in Denver.

On the Par Three, eleventh hole, Bloyer hit one high and far. He and this three playing partners lost sight of the ball due to the bright sun and glare. As they approached the green, Andy Cornell found his ball just ten feet from the cup. Justin Adams spotted his ball just shy of the green in the short rough. Gary Casey would have to play out of a bunker. But where was Casey's ball?

"Maybe it's in the cup," joked Justin.

"Yeah, right," said Casey.

Andy walked over to the cup and took a peek.

"HOLY CRAP, IT'S IN THE CUP! IT'S IN THE CUP!" Cornell screamed with joy.

Casey, Andy, Justin and Gary started jumping up and down celebrating. Casey was having trouble keeping his composure and fell to his knees, tears of joy streaming down his face. He grabbed his cell phone and called his dad with the good news.

"Dad, I did it, I did it!" Casey enthusiastically yelled into the phone.

"Hey, drinks are on you big boy," Gary, who has an ace to his credit, reminded the newest member of the hole-in-one club.

Justin hugged Casey so hard he almost broke the Caseman's ribs.

Finally, Casey walked over to the hole.

"I'm gonna mount the ball on a plaque and put it in my den. Finally! A dream come true."

As Casey leaned over the hole to get the ball he was startled to find the ball wasn't there.

"Andy, did you take the ball?" he asked.

It was then Andy started cracking up uncontrollably. Justin and Gary began laughing so hard they fell to the ground.

Casey was confused by the hysteria. He looked at a nearby groundskeeper.

"Did you see my ball?" Casey asked.

The worker simply pointed to a spot about fifty feet from the green. The ball was behind a tree.

Apparently the celebration of Casey's hole-in-one was a wee bit premature.

THE KICKER

It appeared that it would come down to the right leg of Christo Selmo. A hard fought game amongst behemoths would be decided by the smallest guy on the field, all 5'7 and one-hundred fifty-five pounds of him.

The Dolphins and Chargers were battling for the final wild card playoff spot and tension was off the charts in San Diego.

The Chargers led 30-28, but Miami had the ball and began to march downfield in the final moments as Chad Pennington was hitting his receivers with pinpoint accuracy.

"It looks like the entire season and fate of two teams will come down to Christo Selmo," said play-by-play broadcaster Al Michaels. "Looks like he'll have a chance to make up for that missed 41 yarder in the third quarter."

On the sidelines, Selmo warmed up by kicking balls into the net. Most kickers relish the chance to be a hero. To boot the winning kick through the uprights is what a kicker dreams of. Not Selmo.

He was thinking, "Oh my God. Oh no. Please, please, please don't let it come down to me. We need a touchdown. Even a turnover would be good now. Anything but a kick."

Another first down for the Dolphins. The clock was ticking. They were just about in Selmo's range. The kicker was trying to look calm. While most players stay away from kickers in these situations, a few Dolphins gave the little guy a nod of approval as if to say, "We believe in you. Get the job done."

The TV camera zoomed in for a close-up of Selmo. There he was in his oversized helmet with his single bar face mask trying to look cool and casual. On the outside, Selmo's appearance read, "No big deal. I'll just go in, make the kick, be a hero and get ready for the playoffs. Ho-hum."

On the inside it was quite a different story. Selmo's stomach was queasy. He heard the crowd yelling at him. The man in the number 3 jersey was sweating profusely and was trying not to shake. Nervous and frightened doesn't even begin to describe how Selmo was felt. If he missed the kick it would be a long flight back to Miami and he would be forever remembered as the guy who blew the Dolphins playoff chances. He would be the most hated man in Florida and his hometown of Buenos Aires, Argentina.

With twenty seconds left, Pennington hit tight end Anthony Fasano at the 25 yard line. They were in field goal range with one time out left.

"Oh, crap," thought Selmo.

But then Fasano broke a tackle. He picked up a blocker and ran down the left sideline for a touchdown!

There was jubilation on the Dolphins bench. A relieved Selmo came in and tacked on the extra-point. Miami was going to the playoffs!

In the locker room, a reporter walked up to Selmo and asked him about the win.

"Well," replied the kicker, "I'm really glad we won it, but to be completely honest with you, I really wanted the chance to kick the game winner. I was ready and I would have put it through the uprights no doubt. I'm glad Anthony came up big for us at the end, but I'm confident I would have made the kick if needed. That's my job, that's what I live for."

As Selmo was getting dressed he had this sudden and frightening thought, "The Steelers next week? Oh my God. I hope it doesn't come down to a field goal. Yikes."

MR. INTENSITY

Intense. That was the word that best summed up shortstop Paul Drummond. Whether it was barking at an opposing player, to throw them off their game, brawling with his own "less-intense" teammates, or squawking with umpires, Drummond had one thing on his mind—that was to win at all costs. He wasn't out there to make friends. He was out there to win.

"Intensity doesn't begin to describe Paul," said former teammate Jeremy Weiss. "More like insanity. He was like the modern day Ty Cobb."

Yes, Drummond was called intense. He was also called ferocious, passionate and fiery.

That was forty years ago. Now that he's brought his intense brand of baseball to the little league team he coaches Drummond is no longer called intense, he's simply called—a jerk.

EXCUSE MAKER

The self-proclaimed "Attorney to the Athletes," Arnie Scheinblum was an irritant and nuisance, but somewhat creative when it came to helping athletes come up with excuses when caught using steroids. Scheinblum was always the man they turned to.

"I didn't know steroids were contagious until Jose Canseco coughed on me," said accused cheater Bobby Braywell of the Cubs.

Chargers offensive lineman, Chad Osterbrooks declared, "Since when did Wheaties start putting steroids in their flakes? Man, I'm mad, really, really mad."

Scheinblum also came up with the following classic defense for Red Sox backup infielder Mario Carter.

"How was I to know that the friend of a dentist in California who knew a guy whose uncle in Mexico once played soccer with a guy in Florida who trained greyhounds and knew a guy that worked out of the same gym I did, who recommended that I seek my
workout advice from the very same guy who played soccer in Mexico?" Carter asked, innocently.

After failing a test for performance enhancing substances, Eagles defensive lineman Marquis Beauxmarr added, "I thought I was shooting up heroin, not steroids. I would never knowingly put steroids in my body."

Braves pitcher Bruce Wellborn used a Scheinblum excuse to diminish his shame and grab public sympathy when he claimed, "While walking by a guy playing darts, his errant throw nailed me in the butt. Little did I know it wasn't a dart, but a needle filled with steroids. If it happened to me it can happen to anybody."

Scheinblum told Saints wide receiver Toby Carrington to use the explanation of, "My daughter accidentally injected me with 'roids for a school project although she told me it was B-12." The excuse would have worked better had Carrington actually had a daughter.

Scheinblum gave this classic excuse to Redskins running back Leon Blue, who claimed, "My personal trainer is really a closet Cowboys fan who intentionally injected me with performance enhancing drugs because he wanted me to get suspended to help his team's chances."

Dodgers pitcher Curt Maxwell was coached to say, "It's not my fault. I was dehydrated and in desperation I used Manny Ramirez's urine for the drug test."

Minor league pitcher Chris Cruz, on the advice of Scheinblum, said, "Like so many others, my body naturally produces massive amounts of Winstrol, Decadurbolin, Testosterone and Human Growth Hormone."

Even Pete Rose, who never used performance enhancing drugs during his playing career, said, courtesy of Scheinblum, "Brian McNamee framed Roger Clemens and now he's framing me."

Even though none of Scheinblum's clients have avoided suspensions or punishment the lawyer said, "The objective is to shape public opinion and we're winning that battle. These excuses are all about creating doubt and it works. People are tired of lame excuses like 'The supplement I bought over the counter was tainted'. The more creative the excuse the better the results. Actually, it humors me to no end to find all these dopes who actually buy into these excuses. And I get paid. A lot. Amazing."

A REAL BALLPARK

For years, Earl Stackhouse refused to go to Pirates games at new PNC Park. He only went to a handful of games at the Bucs previous home, Three Rivers Stadium. The main reason why Stackhouse boycotted Pirates games was because he missed old Forbes Field.

"Now that was a ballpark," said Stackhouse.

"Not like these newfangled monstrosities of today."

But on this particular Saturday evening in the Steel City, Stackhouse was about to make good on a promise to his ten-year-old grandson, Timmy, and take him to a Pirates game.

"It's not Forbes Field, but I guess I can deal with it for a few hours," Stackhouse told his daughter Maureen.

As they drove to the stadium and into the nicely paved parking lot, Stackhouse regaled his grandson with stories about fabled Forbes Field.

"The traffic jams were legendary," Stackhouse told Timmy. "The seats were made for real fans, narrow, wooden and uncomfortable. If you were lucky, you didn't get a seat behind a steel beam. The bathrooms were always backing up and the sound system was pretty bad, but it was all about baseball then. No fancy scoreboards, no big concourses or

anything like that. Just baseball and that's the way it should be."

The game began and Timmy was excited as he settled into his comfortable, plush seat. He was wearing the Pirates cap that grandpa bought for him at the gift shop. The beautiful scoreboard, complete with video replay, helped Timmy follow the action. He had a clear view of the field; the green panorama below certainly would become imbedded in Timmy's memory bank forever. He kept score in the glossy Pirates program, packed with information about the team.

Even though the Pirates lost, as usual, it was a fun and memorable night for Timmy and his grandpa.

As the car pulled into the driveway, Timmy said, "Thanks grandpa for taking me to the game. Too bad it wasn't Forbes Field."

Maureen greeted her father when he walked into the house. "So dad, how did you like the new ballpark?"

"Well, it was ok, but it wasn't Forbes Field. Now that was a ballpark!"

A TALE OF TWO STUDENTS

An exuberant crowd was heading towards The Swamp. The Gators were facing LSU in a game with SEC supremacy and BCS implications on the line.

Joe Don Bickerstaff was looking out his dorm room window observing the march to the stadium. The freshman student was wearing a Gators sweatshirt and cap.

"Hey Art," Joe Don asked his roommate Arthur Phillips, a fellow freshman, "you coming to the game this week?"

"Nah, I think I'll skip this one and go to the library," Art said. "I have a paper due next week and I have to do a calc assignment. You have fun."

Joe Don stared at his roommate with disgust and disbelief.

"Art, you haven't been to a game all year," said Bickerstaff. "You didn't know until Thursday that we beat Tennessee last week. I have to ask you man, why the hell did you even bother to come here?"

"I want to get an education," replied Art.

"An education? Then why did you come to Florida?"

"Let me ask you Joe Don, why did you come here?"

"For the football like everyone else. Go Gators!"

With that Joe Don Bickerstaff was off to watch his beloved Gators to be followed by an off-campus party that would end with in typical fashion with J.D. puking in a parking lot or on a sidewalk.

Epilogue

That was ten years ago. Art now works as a chemist for a petroleum company and makes more than a quarter of a million dollars a year.

Joe Don is a seventh year senior at Florida where he still attends games at The Swamp dressed in his orange and blue regalia. He still gets drunk after games and pukes in parking lots and on sidewalks.

CHARLIE

The nurse woke up former high school football star Charlie Greshner at 6 a.m. The normally salty Greshner was quickly put in a good mood when he was told that one-hundred ten-year-old Frank Menninger passed away at an assisted living center in Clearwater, Florida.

Menninger's passing meant that Charlie Greshner, at one-hundred nine years, four months and twenty-two days was the world's oldest human.

"It's about time that old geezer kicked it," said Greshner. "I've been waiting for this for a long time."

There was a celebration that afternoon at the Stricker Nursing Home in Maywood, New Jersey.

"I'm so happy for Charlie," said Amelia Traber, a ninety-six-year-old who lives down the hall from Greshner. "Every day he would say, 'I hope that old bastard Menninger kicks the bucket today.' Well, his dream has finally come true. What a competitor!"

One of the nurses, Denise Fisher was glad to hear the news too. "I think that the reason Charlie has lived so long is because one of his goals was to become the oldest person in the world. Now that's he's finally accomplished that he'll probably …you know, probably, like …um, well I have to go to Mrs. Heidelberg's room now."

Meanwhile, eight days later at a rest home in Kentucky …"Mr. H," nurse Catherine Klein said to one-hundred eight-year-old Thomas Horvath, "We have some good news out of New Jersey today. …"

STRIGHT TALK

"I can't understand it," Bernard Waltham said to his friend Bryan Kersey. "I'm a champion athlete, yet nobody knows who I am. What is wrong?"

"Well, Bernie, it takes time," Bryan responded. "They'll know all about you soon enough."

"Come on Bryan, that's not true. I've been at this for twenty years. Level with me, what's the problem."

"You want it straight?"

"Yeah, give it to me straight."

"Well, ok. Bernie, you are a shot putter. A shot putter. Nobody cares about the shot put or that you hold records."

"Really? I don't believe that."

"Yeah, really. Basically you heave around a cannon ball. There's no strategy. There's no drama. Even when you set that record last year nobody cared. Why? Because it's shot putting, that's why. You moan about not getting women. Well look at you. Only big fat guys are good at the shot put. Name one guy in decent shape who was a great shot putter? I'll help you out—none. Your social skills have also been stunted because all you do is lift weights and train to throw that stupid fourteen pound ball."

"Sixteen pounds."

"Ok, sixteen pounds. Whatever. The only sixteen pound balls people are interested in are bowling balls or elephant balls. So you throw this cannonball around and you get excited when you throw it one inch more than you did the last time. Guess what Bernie, nobody freaking cares! Shot putting is boring. It's stupid. It's a colossal waste of time and has absolutely no redeeming social value."

Bryan didn't want to rip apart his friend but he was on a roll. "Even ESPN doesn't want to put it on TV because the only people watching are only fellow shot putters or people who feel sorry for shot putters. The only reason I watch you and your moronic shot putting events is because we grew up together and our families our close. I feel obligated. If I don't watch that crap, who will?"

Bernie was sitting on the couch with his head in his massive, calcified hands. Perhaps it was true what Bryan was saying.

But Bryan wasn't finished. He stood facing the trophy case, turned and resumed his tirade. "So basically Bernie, nobody likes the shot put, nobody cares about the shot put and shot putters are usually disgusting fat guys and that's why they can't land a date, something you are experiencing now. Lose the shot put, drop some weight, clean up your act and maybe, just maybe you'll get laid. Anyway, I don't mean to be harsh Bernie but you wanted me to give it to you straight. So, there you have it. Hey, let's go grab some lunch."

Bernie didn't respond. He was staring out the window and knew, deep down in his heart, that Bryan was right. Bernie also realized, too late, that he should have thrown the discus.

THE WATER COOLER

"Good morning Chuck, how goes?" asked Tim as he walked into the break room at the office.

"Stressed out Tim, stressed out," was Chuck's reply as he sipped a cup of coffee.

"Why's that?"

"Man, I'm really torn about tonight's Packers-Chiefs game and the Jets-Saints game. I like the Packers getting three, but I'm not sure how long Rodgers will play. Plus, the Chiefs have been getting some inconsistent play out of their offensive line. As for the Jets game, I'm thinking of taking the under. Both teams have been inconsistent on offense and Brees is likely to just go a quarter for the Saints. But I'm trying to figure out the approach that Sean Payton will take for the Saints."

"Wait, let me get this right Chuck, you're betting on exhibition football?"

"Actually it's called pre-season football."

"Ok, pre-season football. You're betting on pre-season football?"

"Uh, yeah. Don't you?"

"No I don't Chuck."

With that Tim handed a business card to Chuck.

"Here, take this. This is a good friend of mine. Give him a call today."

Chuck looked at the card and shrugged his shoulders. It simply said, "Dr. Mark Avery, Mental Health Specialist, 888-888-5150."

At lunchtime, Tim strolled into the break room. He glanced into the wastepaper basket. Inside was Dr. Avery's business card.

Come the next morning, Chuck would be out another two-hundred bucks.

THE SET-UP

Davey "Ruptured Spleen" Green began his professional boxing career with an 0-12 record. He was knocked out in all twelve bouts.

His manager, Nick Vella, was concerned. "Kid," said Vella, "we gotta set you up with a tomata can. Once you get that first win you'll be on your way. Get it?"

Green nodded in agreement.

Trainer Hipolito Maldonado asked, "Who you got in mind Nicky?"

Vella pondered the question for a moment and then said, "Hey, what about digging up Johnny Carello?"

Maldonado replied, "But ain't he dead? Didn't they find his body in Secaucus last year?"

Vella was quiet for a moment, flashed a devious smile, leaned forward and said softly, "Exactly."

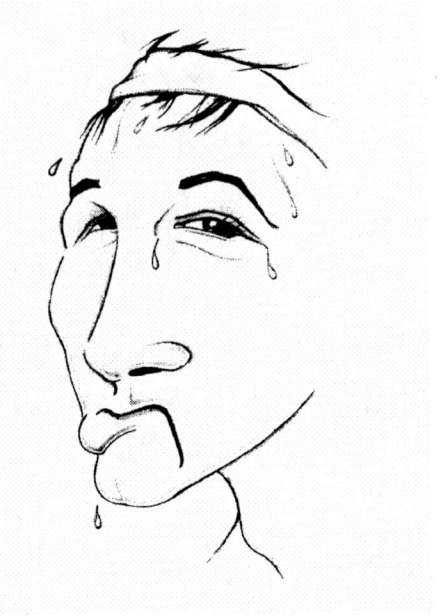

THE MARATHONER

Todd Weaver always dreamed of running a marathon. He called it the ultimate personal challenge.

A week after completing the 2009 Chicago Marathon, Weaver was singing a different tune.

"It was the dumbest thing I've ever done," said the 35-year-old graphic artist. "My body is in severe pain. I can't even get out of bed."

Weaver's wife Cassandra isn't sympathetic to her husband's plight. "I told him it was foolish to run a marathon," she said. "He's not an athlete. But does he listen? No. His training consisted of running to the fridge to get a beer or chasing the cat in the backyard."

"It was a horrible experience," Weaver said. "I was in excruciating pain at mile three and I got the splats at mile seventeen. I've learned my painful lesson. People are not supposed to run marathons."

Weaver, however, is a man in constant search of challenges. His next goal is to compete in the Ironman Triathlon in Hawaii in January.

"Hey man, I can do it. I ran a marathon you know," he said while holding his side.

GAME, SET, BROKEN FACE

Gabe Wasserman was never so happy to lose a tennis match. The 53-year-old IT technician was playing for the club championship, but lost a five-set heartbreaker to 53-year-old Randy Blair.

As soon as the cocky Blair zipped a forehand winner down the sideline for the match, he went to congratulate Wasserman.

"I was disappointed to lose the championship for the third consecutive year, especially to a schmuck like Randy," recalled Wasserman. "But in retrospect, I'm glad I did."

Blair went to leap the net to shake hands with Wasserman and rub some salt in his wounds but instead caught his toe on the three-foot high barrier.

The resulting face plant accomplished two things. It gave the chirpy Blair a fractured nose and jaw, much to the delight of Wasserman. It also gave Wasserman an idea.

"I figured that a lot of older idiots try to jump the net but don't get high enough to clear it anymore," explained Wasserman. "So, I invented the mechanical net where once a match is finished, someone just has to press a button to lower the net to either two feet or one foot, depending upon the leaping ability, or lack thereof, of the leaper. This invention is going to make me millions! All because Randy Blair was being a jackass and tried to jump the net."

While this invention will revolutionize tennis, according to its inventor, the fact remains, not one company has offered to buy Wasserman's patent.

"It's just a matter of time, that's all. A matter of time," Wasserman said.

THE MEETING

The note, delivered to the football coach, by a secretary, was simple and to the point. It read, "Coach, please be advised that you are required to be in attendance at an emergency meeting Thursday morning at nine o'clock in the office of the University President."

The prestigious Southeastern Conference school president had summoned the head coach to his office.

Several key members of the board were also on hand. The meeting was kept quiet from the rest of the faculty, athletic department, students and media.

The coach wondered what the meeting was about. It couldn't be too bad he thought. As a matter of fact, he believed it would be about a contract extension.

Four bowl games in five seasons and an overall record of 43-21 was pretty good. It wasn't National Championship good, but the coach was pleased with the direction of the program.

When he arrived at the clandestine meeting he immediately knew something was wrong.

"Coach, this isn't going to be easy, but we need some answers from you," began the President. "We were looking at your overall body of work when it came to my attention, that under your stewardship, there have been no major or minor violations in your program."

Suddenly the nervous coach felt his spirits pick up. "That is correct sir," replied the coach.

"Furthermore," continued the President, "there have been no in-house investigations or allegations leveled against your program's recruiting practices. In your prior head coaching position, there were no NCAA violations of any kind. Am I correct in that statement?"

"That is true," the coach responded.

"Let me ask you this coach—what the hell is going on? Are you even trying? This is the SEC! We aren't like other leagues or schools, except for that damn Vanderbilt program and I ain't seen no championship flags flying over at their stadium. Let me tell you this, we can't compete for National Championships with this kind of recruiting."

The coach was fuming and said, "With all due respect, I run a squeaky clean program and recruit good kids with solid backgrounds who are students first and foremost."

"And that's the problem," said the President. "If you want to keep your job then you better start recruiting the way other schools in this league do. If the NCAA comes sticking their noses in our business, we'll back you all the way, y'all hear?"

After an awkward moment of silence the coach nodded his head. The meeting was over.

A year later, the school was hit with major NCAA violations for illegal recruiting practices.

"I am disappointed and shocked at the violations in our football program," the President told the media. "We pride ourselves on following the rules and it's a shame that a renegade, win at all costs coach has besmirched this institution's reputation. We have fired the coach and have hired a new football coach, a man of exemplary character. ..."

TERM PAPERS

B+. Despite all the work and effort Charlotte Smith put into her term paper on the "History of Western Civilization" she still got a damn B+. The straight "A" English major was incensed.

"I can't believe I got a B+," Smith told her classmate LaMarcus McKinney. "I worked so hard on that paper. That's the first time I didn't get an "A". How about you LaMarcus, did you get a passing grade?"

"Yeah, I got a A+," replied McKinney.

"You? You got an A+?"

"Yeah."

"Do you have your paper with you?"

"Yeah, it's right here."

The paper was clearly marked. Sure enough it said, "A+".

Charlotte was too polite to say it, but she was thinking, "You are dumber than a doorknob. You rarely bother to show up to class. You can barely talk. How the hell did you get an A+?"

She opened the paper to the first page and read it to herself.

It read, "The History of Westin Civilisation by LaMarcus McKinney. Civilisations grew in history because the womens be having lots of kids. Those kids than had kids and stuff like that. Then there was some societys that had wars wit other societys and they created there own countrees. One day Columbus got on his boat wit other peeps and they sailed to the United States where they got rid of the Indians cause they didn't smoke no peace pipe or nothing like that. Soon George Washington was the president and he was the man in charge and ..."

Charlotte had seen enough. She handed the paper back to LaMarcus.

"Pretty good wasn't it?" asked LaMarcus.

"Yes, LaMarcus, it was good. I'm happy for you."

"Thanks. So you be going to the game Saturday?"

"Yes, I'll be there. Good luck."

With that, Charlotte strolled back to her dorm room before heading to her on-campus job. LaMarcus headed over to football practice.

In three days Charlotte Smith would be just one of ninety-thousand people cheering for her school as well as All-America running back and future NFL first round draft pick LaMarcus McKinney.

SCORING MORE POINTS MILESTONE

"Ahh, Coach, what will be the keys to victory on Saturday against Purdue?" asked reporter Sid LaBarr.

"Scoring more points," was Michigan State Head Coach Mark Dantonio's slick response.

Little did he know it but Dantonio's 'scoring more points' line was the 1,000,000th time a coach has used that phrase.

Media historian Ross Unruh said, "It was funny the first time that line was used when Knute Rockne was being interviewed by newspaper columnist Grantland Rice during Notre Dame's undefeated season in 1919. Since then, not so funny."

Sportscaster Bob Behler said, "The funny thing about coaches dropping the lame 'scoring more points' line is that they actually think they are being clever. If Rockne trademarked that line his family would have made a fortune. That would have been the smart thing for 'The Rock' to do. Certainly smarter than being a passenger on a wooden plane in a lightning storm over Kansas."

When told by LaBarr that he dropped the 'scoring more points' phrase for the 1,000,000th time in coaching lingo history, Dantonio said, "Really. I just take it one quote at a time and good Lord willing we will score more points Saturday. So, if you ask me another weak 'what are the keys to victory' question I'll drop the 'scoring more points' line again. And again. And again. Then I'll kick your ass. Now get out of my office."

UPON FURTHER REVIEW

Yale Head Coach Raymond "Ducky" Pond was furious. The Princeton receiver clearly was juggling the ball when he went out of bounds in front of the Yale bench; however, the side judge ruled it a good catch.

Pond threw a red flag on the field and called for the referee.

"What's this red flag about? What do you want Ducky?" asked the ref.

"The receiver didn't have possession of the ball."

"Not my call."

"I want a review."

"A What?"

"I want you to call up to the replay booth and take another look at the play. He was bobbling the ball and when you see it again you'll reverse the call."

The referee looked strangely at Pond.

"You OK Ducky?"

"I'm fine. I want that play reviewed in the booth damn it!"

The ref shrugged his shoulders and went back to his position on the field.

"What the hell was he yapping about?" asked the line judge.

"Ducky is a little crazy," said the referee.

The game continued and Yale eventually defeated Princeton 7-0, ending the Tigers 15 game winning streak.

This occurred on November 17, 1934.

Yes, Ducky Pond was a coach ahead of his time.

VALENTINA THE AVENGER

After a cat-fight backstage during a fashion show, super model Valentina Van Dortmond decided it would be a good idea to learn proper fighting techniques.

She always knew she had to keep in shape for her career. Why not ditch swimming and some of her other aerobic exercises for a while to cross-train at the boxing gym?

While she stood out like a fully dressed Eskimo at a nudist colony, Valentina enjoyed learning how to box at the Times Square Gym in New York. She became somewhat proficient at hitting the speed bag and heavy bag. She learned proper footwork and how to punch and counterpunch.

Her trainer, Maxey Dunn, 75, came to the conclusion that it might be fun for Valentina to step into the ring for a real fight.

"I don't know Maxey," Valentina told the grizzled trainer. "I'm a model. I need to look good."

Dunn pondered the situation and said, "Don't worry, you're doing great. I'll set you up with some girl who you can beat easily."

After some trepidation, Valentina reluctantly agreed to give it a shot. The night of the fight came.

Valentina was nervous.

"Your opponent is some girl named Brown." Dunn told her. "You can handle her easy. Just stick and move and you'll be fine kid."

The crowd at Madison Square Garden settled in for the Van Dortmond-Brown undercard bout.

Valentina was tense, but confident. Until she heard

the ring announcer.

"In the red corner, weighing in at one-hundred twenty-one pounds, from Oslo, Norway, fighting out of the Times Square Gym, making her professional debut, Valentinaaaaaa Van Dortmond! In the blue corner, from Brooklyn, New York, fighting out of Gleason's Gym, and weighing in at one-hundred twenty-five pounds, with a professional record of 38-0, the North American Allied Champeen, LaShanique "Put You Down" Brooooooown!"

The bell rang and in short order Valentina had her nose broken and her mouth bloodied. The carnage lasted all of forty-three seconds. Brown remained undefeated and Valentina decided to end her boxing career, although she wanted one more fight. The next day, Valentina showed up at the Time Square Gym. She climbed into a ring where Dunn was training a fighter.

"Excuse me," the facially bruised Valentina said to the young fighter.

It was there that Dunn got the beating of a lifetime as Valentina ran her record to 1-1 before officially hanging up the gloves.

TAKING INVENTORY

Teddy was exhausted as he sat on the edge of his bed in another non-descript hotel room in another city he couldn't remember.

He fell back on the bed and stared at the ceiling. He missed his wife and kids. He even missed his dog. He missed everything about being at home. His own bed and showering in his own bathroom. Another road trip and another week away from the people he loved.

It was a difficult lifestyle. He thought of the memories he would never have because he was on the road, like missed birthdays and barbeques, time on the beach and school plays and concerts. Doubt was creeping into his mind.

"Is this all worth it?" he wondered. "Am I a good father and husband?"

He flipped on the television. Baseball highlights were being shown. He saw himself belt a three-run homer that won that night's game.

A few moments later, room service arrived followed by a call from a special lady friend.

He also reminded himself that he was making fourteen million dollars a season.

Orioles outfielder Teddy McCormick came to the conclusion, "Yes it's worth it, oh hell yes!"

WEST COAST OFFENSE

Coach Jordy Maples had seen enough, after a disappointing 2-9 season.

"This off-season we have to change the offense," Maples told his assistant coaches. "We need to install the West Coast offense."

Maples spent the next several months going to coaching clinics, reading coaching manuals and watching films. He was ready to implement a highly sophisticated West Coast offense.

After the first three games of the new season, Coach Maples was stunned. His West Coast offense scored zero points in three games.

"I don't get it," Maples lamented to assistant coach Brian Taylor. "I mean, we've gone over this time and bleeping time again. And the guys can't seem to pick it up. I knew there would be growing pains, but this is ridiculous. What the hell is the problem Brian?"

Taylor tried to be as tactful as possible, but he also had to be honest. "Jordy, the playbook is 446 pages long. This is an offense that is difficult to grasp for the pros and college guys so maybe our seven and eight-year-olds need more time to digest it. Also, it might help if our quarterback could throw the ball more than three yards past the line of scrimmage."

Maples thought about it and reached the conclusion that Taylor was out of his mind and fired him as assistant coach for the Denver Demons of the Mile High Pee Wee Football League.

THE GRANITE BOWL

With the addition of the Granite Bowl to the college football post-season landscape, there are now 58 college football bowl games. The result is that of the 117 Division One football teams, all but one will be participating in a bowl game.

The Granite Bowl will be played in Hanover, New Hampshire on December 23rd, at 20,000 seat Memorial Field on the campus of Dartmouth College.

"Just because Ivy League football teams aren't Division One and can't go to bowl games doesn't mean we can't host a bowl game," said Dartmouth Athletic Director Bob Ceplikas. "We're pumped! Actually I'm obligated to say we're pumped."

New Hampshire Governor John Lynch, not to be confused with the long-time NFL safety of the same name, said, "We needed a centerpiece event here in New Hampshire to remind people in America that we are still one of the fifty states in this great land. Now we have that marquee event."

The Granite Bowl will pit the number ten team in the Big 12 against the number nine team in the Western Athletic Conference.

"I've always been a big fan of Louisiana Tech," said Governor Lynch. "I'm secretly hoping they finish ninth in the WAC this year. Although now I guess that secret is out."

Hanover resident Alan Jepperson was in favor of the bowl game coming to his hometown. "Hell, if Grand Forks, Minnesota (The Freezer Bowl) and Buckhannon, West Virginia (The Hillbilly Bowl) can have bowl games, why not us?"

Of course with any venture of this magnitude there will be some obstacles to overcome.

Granite Bowl committee chairman Brett Davis said, "First of all we had to insure a lucrative payoff to not only the teams, but the NCAA honchos who approve of bowl games. Those bastards are shakedown artists, let me tell you. Anyway, we rustled up some sponsorship dollars from the local Hanover businesses and each team will get a payout of five-thousand dollars. Next, we had to find some really ugly blazers for the bowl committee members. That was pretty easy actually. Finally, we had to have a Granite Bowl trophy. We overspent our budget on that one because the original trophy, made of granite, weighed 2,400 pounds or basically as much as former Kansas Coach Mark Mangino. So, we decided to go for the replica plastic trophy which kind of looks like granite, or melted linoleum."

NCAA spokesperson Melanie Mayfield said, "This is a wonderful opportunity to allow two more teams to experience participating in a bowl game and take advantage of the cultural aspects of New Hampshire, whatever they may be. Granted, they'll be two lousy teams, but more football is good, isn't it? Unfortunately, one poor team will be left out of the bowl picture, but we have a couple of options. We can give them a trophy that shows they achieved the distinction of being the absolute worst team in college football. Or we can create a bowl game for them. Perhaps call it the 'Intra-Squad Bowl' and they can play it on their campus."

The Granite Bowl will be aired on QVC, The Home Shopping Network, where fans will be able to purchase Granite Bowl merchandise. Tickets are on sale now at www.horriblebowlgame.com.

NO GO FOR RANGOON

"I can't believe it. I can't believe it," said Rangoon Olympic Committee Chairman Naishwe Muong. "Rio de Janeiro? What do they have that we don't have? I just can't believe the International Olympic Committee didn't select our country."

While the city of Rio de Janeiro and Brazil celebrated the awarding of the 2016 Olympic Games, Rangoon and its suppressed residents suffered.

"We have some of the best government corruption in the entire world," Muong added. "We have rundown soccer stadiums that with a little paint would be more than adequate to host the games. We have unsafe drinking water, a monsoon season that would coincide with the games, high crime and prostitution, diseases and a heavy handed military that can maim and torture with the best of them. We put the goon in Rangoon!" The diminutive chairman continued his diatribe, waving his arms wildly, as his secretary cowered under her desk. "Throw in our horrible human rights record and government run propagandized media and our bid for the Olympics was second to none. People are going to die over this. People are going to die."

When asked why Rio de Janeiro got the games over Rangoon, IOC spokesperson Lenard Valasky said, "Well, every country that bid for the games finished ahead of Rangoon. Let's be honest here, Rangoon's bribes didn't come close to those of Rio and the other countries. Plus, Rio has topless beaches! Have you seen what Rangoonian women look like? Now if you'll excuse me, I'm going to hit some Swedish and Norwegian delegates up for money for the next winter games."

THEM'S THE BREAKS

The ball was hit sharply to Dave Powers. The All-Star shortstop was in position to make the play and send the Orioles to the playoffs for the first time in fourteen years. But the ball went through Powers's legs and the tying and go-ahead runs scored. In the bottom of that inning, Powers, with a chance to redeem himself, hit into a bases loaded game-ending double play. Just like that, the dream was over as the capacity crowd at Camden Yards silently filed out of the stadium. The season was done and Powers was the goat.

"You gotta feel bad for the guy," said season ticket holder Antonio Jarboe. "I mean, we wouldn't have even gotten this close without him. I feel sorry for him."

Another fan, Rhonda Jardine, said, "I feel so bad for Dave. I want to give him a big hug."

True baseball fans could certainly feel Dave's pain. Orioles Manager Dave Trembley quietly told the media, "That's baseball. It can be a cruel game. I just hope Dave recovers after this."

Baltimore announcer Jim Palmer said, "This was a tough way to lose a game. I don't think Powers will ever get over this. His career will be defined by this miscue like Bill Buckner or Ralph Branca."

In the clubhouse, Powers was forlorn and downtrodden. His teammates felt badly for Powers, but were glad it was him and not them to blow the game. Nobody wants to be the goat.

Following a shower and uncomfortable post-game interviews, Powers got into his $470,000 silver 2009 Maybach and drove to his in-season mansion on Gibson

Island.

The next day Powers was chauffeured to his private jet at the Carroll County Airport for the flight to his 1,500 acre ranch in Texas. After spending a couple of days hunting and fishing on his property, he and his wife Wendi, a former Cowboys cheerleader, headed to their private Caribbean retreat. But it wasn't all rest and relaxation for Powers. While on his 80 foot yacht, he was engaged in conversations with his agent Scott Boras.

Powers, heading into the last year of a four year, 48-million dollar contract, would be a free-agent after next season and Boras was outlining a plan that could bring him a bigger deal than the one he signed with Baltimore. There were also the typical off-season endorsement deal headaches to discuss.

After docking in Aruba and dining at a magnificent resort restaurant, Powers and his wife took a stroll on the beach.

It wasn't long after when a fan recognized the shortstop and said, "Hey Dave, you're my favorite player. Hey, can I get a picture with you?"

"Sure, no problem buddy," said Powers.

After the picture was taken, the fan said, "Thanks. And hey man, sorry about the error last week."

"Thanks," said Dave.

A few moments later, Dave turned to Wendi and asked, "What error?"

His wife shrugged and said, "I wasn't really listening. I was too busy looking at my new diamond ring."

Yes, baseball fans everywhere felt bad for Dave Powers. Not one of them would want to be in his shoes.

Yep, it would tragic to be Dave Powers.

TULO'S LUNCH

Troy Tulowitzki was enjoying lunch at the Coronado Café before that night's game against the Diamondbacks. The Rockies shortstop's pleasant, relaxing afternoon was interrupted by a phone call.

"Hello," said Tulowitzki.

"Is this Troy?" asked the caller.

"Yeah, who's this?"

"Never mind who this is. The question is, what the hell is going on out there? I mean come on Tulo, I paid a lot of money for you and this is the return on my investment, a .224 average over the past ten games with just one homer and four RBI's? Are you kidding me?"

"Well, it's just a small slump. I'm doing everything I can to get back on track."

"Everything? And what are you doing now? Are you taking early B.P. or extra video work? No, you are sitting in your hotel room watching TV."

"Actually, I'm eating lunch."

"Quiet, I'm talking here. I'm counting on you Tulo. I need you to start coming through. I don't want to bench you or trade you or even send you to the minors."

"The minors? Are you serious Mr. Monfort?"

"Monfort?"

"Yeah, isn't this Mr. Monfort?"

"No, this is Jim Roser owner of the Santé Fe Diablos. You're on my fantasy team and I'm really upset that …"

CLICK.

Tulo sat at the restaurant and had a fantasy of his own. That was to see all fantasy nutcases go away—far, far away.

SHOULDA WORN HEADGEAR

During high school it was cool. In college it was a badge of honor. But following his wrestling career and inability to land a date, Ken Wilson came to the sad and startling conclusion: "Cauliflower ears suck."

DEDUCTIVE REASONING

Phil was reading the newspaper in the living room of his Ocean City, New Jersey home while his wife was glancing at a magazine.

"Hey Emily, did you hear that Donald Trump wants to bring a Major League baseball team to Atlantic City?"

"Really? That could be interesting" she said.

"What does the story say?"

"Well, Trump wants to build a three-billion dollar stadium called Trump Park, then he wants to bring in a team and call them the Jersey Trumps. The team will have cheerleaders called the Trumpettes and they'll serve Trump Dogs and Trump Ale to the fans. The mascot will be named Trumpy and get this, he'll have a train called the Trump Tram that will allow people to travel from Trump Park to the Trump Casinos. The stadium is also going to have a giant video board called Trumpvision that he said would make the video board at the Cowboys new stadium look like a hand held screen. This entire thing sounds pretty impressive. What do you think?"

Emily mulled over the question then said, "I think Donald has a small wanker."

STAYING ALIVE

He was born on the north side of Chicago in January of 1909, just a few months following the Cubs second consecutive World Series victory over the Tigers.

Life was tough for Leo Corrigan growing up. His dad died in a train accident when Leo was seven. His mom, who was frequently ill, worked two jobs to raise her four children and put food on the table. When Leo was ten, he worked various jobs, such as shining shoes or selling newspapers to help the family out.

As a teenager he saved enough money to go to Northwestern University, but then the depression hit and he had to scrap those plans to help out the family.

Eventually he met a woman, Gertrude, who he married in 1936. Unfortunately she died in November of 1938 from influenza. He never married again. He simply went on with his life, working mostly as a laborer.

While Leo never had it easy and experienced his share of family tragedies he always had his beloved Cubs. They were his salvation.

Leo went to Wrigley Field as often as possible. Sometimes with friends, sometimes by himself. Ever the optimist, Leo always thought, "This is our year, this is the year we win the (bleeping) World Series."

There were massive disappointments. In 1969 the Cubs blew a large lead and lost out to the Mets.

"Can you believe that?" Leo said. "The stinking Mets. We had Banks, Santo, Williams, Fergie and we lost to those douchebags? Unbelievable. Damn that was tough."

In 1984, after grabbing a two games to none playoff lead on the Padres, the Cubs lost the next three in San

Diego.

"Lee Smith gave up a game winning homer to (bleeping) Garvey. How about the ball that took a bad hop over Sandberg's head? I'll never forgive (bleeping) Durham for letting the ball go through his legs. That was awful. (Bleep)."

Recalling the 2003 playoffs brought the grizzled Corrigan to tears. "Bartman. (Bleeping) Bartman. (Bleep) that guy. If I wasn't so old I'd track him down and beat his (bleeping) ass."

Time marches on for all including Leo.

"I'm around 100-years-old," Leo said. "But I made a promise to myself to live long enough to see the (bleeping) Cubbies win the Series."

Doctor Michael Erdek has cared for Leo Corrigan for many years. "He's beaten every illness he's had," said Dr. Erdek. "He should have been dead years ago. But he's on a quest is to see the Cubs win the World Series in his lifetime and he refuses to die. When I told him a decade ago that he had several forms of inoperable cancer throughout his body, he laughed and said, 'To hell with cancer. Who's pitching today for the Cubs?' He's alive simply because the Cubs have been hapless for a century."

"Mr. Corrigan can't remember what he had for lunch. But he can rattle off every detail of the 1945 World Series," Nurse Eleanor Haverman said. "He can tell you every stat of Aramis Ramirez. He's obsessed with the Cubs and won't die until they win the World Series. The guy could live another hundred years the way it's going."

Leo Corrigan continues to beat the odds, staying alive just to see the Cubs win a World Series. It must be torture to be Leo Corrigan.

Epilogue

A look into the Turf Tales crystal ball shows that the Cubs won the World Series on October 26th, 2033, defeating the Athletics. Leo Corrigan died on October 29th, 2033 at the age of one-hundred twenty-four. He was (bleeping) happy.

SHE'S A LADY

The weary traveler exited his cheap motel room, got into his rental car and headed down the street to the local watering hole. He figured he'd have a beer or two before bed and then be on his way to his next appointment the following day.

While sipping his beer he noticed a trashy looking blonde at the end of the bar.

Craig was feeling a little frisky and thought, "She looks pretty easy. Why not?"

After engaging in small talk, he convinced the harsh looking woman to take him back to her place.

They drove up to her trailer home and went inside. The light was low and Craig made his move.

BAM! An uppercut to the jaw knocked Craig down. Then a lamp was busted over his head, opening up a six-inch gash.

"What the hell are you doing," yelled Craig.

"Shut your (bleeping) face," the woman screamed back as she kicked Craig in the face with her steel-toed boot.

Craig tried to get up off the floor, but couldn't after the woman jumped on his back and put him in a headlock. She then banged his head against the bottom of the dresser several times.

After she let him up, Craig staggered a bit and then lunged at the woman. She sidestepped him and then when Craig turned around she popped him in the nose, a perfect right cross. Blood rushed out of his broken beak.

She then took an iron and threw it at him, nailing him in the head. Still woozy, Craig stayed on his feet and threw a wild punch at the woman. It missed. Then he felt a baseball bat crush his ribs. He went down. She kicked him again and again and again.

He finally was able to crawl to the doorway and then she kicked him again for good measure as he fell out of the trailer, down the steps onto the dirt. He was covered in blood, his clothes ripped apart and his head was hurting like it had never hurt before. He was also missing some teeth.

The moral of the story—Don't mess with Tonya Harding.

POOR CAREER CHOICE

They display their under-appreciated athletic abilities with theatrical flair to thousands of people. To an outsider they look happy, content and satisfied. But those who know the truth are aware of the sad fact that rodeo clowns are an unhappy bunch.

Legendary rodeo clown Lucky Bucky, real name Jimmy Meyer, says, "As a kid I admired rodeo clowns. It looked like they had it all. I had a choice to make, college or rodeo clown school. Well, here I am, living in poverty, working in dirt and jumping in barrels to escape angry bulls. Sometimes the bull wins."

Veteran rodeo clown Dwayne Shaw sat in his dilapidated trailer lamenting the way his life has turned out. "There is no union for rodeo clowns. There are no benefits unless you like getting kicked in the head by a horse or steer. The glory? Well, it's not what it once was."

Shaw took a sip of coffee and continued. "In my early days of rodeo clowning, I was respected. But now? Well, we get looked at as freaks. Nobody finds rodeo clowns entertaining anymore. My ex-wife and three kids left me because they were tired of people always asking, 'So, where's the rodeo clown these days?' Trust me, I made a poor career choice."

Another long-time rodeo clown, Jeff "Slappy" Moody, says, "I dropped out of medical school for this? I thought I could make a difference as a rodeo clown, but that's not the case." There was a forlorn look on his face and his eyes were misty. "People don't laugh with me, they laugh at me. They look at me like I'm some sort of clown—which I guess I am. I made a bad career choice, but, at least I don't work in the radio industry."

DEMO TAPE

Prior to his play-by-play assignment, the eager broadcaster spoke to the studio engineer.

"Dave, please do me a favor and tape the game for me," the broadcaster said. "Also, can we meet sometime next week so you can help me with my demo tape?"

"Yeah, no problem. What about the demo we made three weeks ago?"

"Well, it was okay but I want to update it. You know, keep it fresh."

"Do you really think you need another demo tape?"

"Absolutely. You never know. There are a lot of broadcasters who would want my job. Plus, what if I get fired tomorrow? I'll need a fresh tape."

He knew he had to be on top of his game and not to take the broadcast for granted.

With that, Vin Scully settled in to call another Dodgers game, something he has been doing since 1950. And he was on top of his game, as usual.

IT'S ALL IN THE WOOD

Chuck bought a cheap piece of wood and brought it home. He took out his lathe and started to carve out a baseball bat.

After sanding and varnishing it, Chuck had himself a nice looking, lightweight, thirty-three inch baseball bat.

He burned a label onto the bat and engraved his name on the barrel. It looked just like a Louisville Slugger.

The next step was to use it in a game.

Chuck stepped up to the plate for his summer league team.

The pitcher delivered a pitch to Chuck that looked appealing. Chuck took a mighty swing and hit the ball squarely, right on the barrel.

The bat shattered into a million pieces and the ball feebly rolled back to the pitcher. Chuck was thrown out at first and was heartbroken that his bat was now nothing but splinters.

When he got back to the bench one of his teammates, Ted Stavish, gave Chuck some sage advice. "You know Chuck, maybe the next time you decide to make a bat, you should spring for ash or maple and not balsa."

A CRUEL WAY TO GO

Sean McCallister wasn't feeling very well, and it had nothing to do with the drubbing the Red Sox were taking at Fenway Park.

His hands felt numb and he was chilly despite the warm temperatures. His wife Alison suggested they leave the game early and plan to go see Doctor O'Hearn the next day.

The following morning, Sean was put through a multitude of tests and was instructed to return the following week, which he did.

"The test results are in Sean," the doctor told him. "And, I'm afraid I have some bad news."

"Oh no," said Alison.

Sean stared at the floor and then looked up. "Well, what is it doc?" he asked.

"I'm afraid Sean that you have a fatal illness for which there is no cure."

"You're afraid? I'm the one who should be afraid."

"But it gets worse Sean."

"Worse?"

"Yes, worse. You only have a few months to a year to live."

Sean sat silently while tears were streaming down Alison's face.

Doctor O'Hearn broke the silence with another declaration. "It gets even worse than that Sean."

"Worse than having a fatal illness that will kill me within a year? How can anything be worse than that?"

"Well Sean, you're a huge Red Sox fan right?"

"Of course. What does that have to do with

anything?"

"Hear me out Sean. You also hate the Yankees right?"

"Absolutely. I hate that team with all my heart. But forget that for now. What could be worse than what you've told me?"

"Well, Sean, I'll give it to you straight if you'd like."

"Come on Doc, tell me."

"Ok Sean. I don't know how to say this, but well, you have the worst disease a Red Sox fan could get?"

"What are you talking about Doc?"

"Sean, you have Lou Gehrig's disease."

ONE DAY PERHAPS

After being retired from coaching for many years, 73-year-old Dan Hawkins has made a return to the sidelines.

The former Boise State and Colorado head coach is now coaching ninth graders at Holy Family High School in Broomfield, Colorado.

"I missed coaching and I'm looking forward to helping the coaches and great kids here at Holy Family," said the still youthful looking Hawkins.

Running back Joe Connelly said, "I had never heard of Coach Hawkins, but he fired us up the first day of practice when he said, 'This ain't pee wee football, this ain't Pop Warner football, THIS IS NINTH GRADE FRESHMEN HIGH SCHOOL FOOTBALL. IT'S THE FRONT RANGE LEAGUE!"

Linebacker Rob Watkins enjoys playing for Hawkins. "Yeah he's tough, but that's the way we like it. One kid complained that practice was too hard and Coach Hawk said, 'Go play intramurals brother, go play intramurals' and I thought that was a little harsh, but funny."

THE VISITOR

With his long-haul truck out of commission for a few days, Warren Bechter was stranded in Denver.

While inconvenient, it certainly beat being stuck in Detroit or Oakland.

The 47-year-old driver decided to make the best of his time and take in a baseball game at beautiful Coors Field.

The hefty Bechter, his shirt already sporting mustard stains, settled into his seat and immediately felt uncomfortable. He couldn't put his finger on it.

In the second inning he turned to a fan, Ed Henderson, sitting next to him in the lower level behind the third base dugout.

"Hey pal, what's with these people?"

Ed, decked out in a Rockies cap and shirt said, "What do you mean?"

"Well," said Bechter, "How come no one is yelling crap at the other team?"

"Yelling crap at the other team?"

"Yeah, like this: HEY REYNOLDS, YOU SUCK! YOU'RE A PIECE OF $%#%$$&#$^&!!!"

People sitting near Bechter were appalled and shot him disapproving glances.

"We don't do that here," replied Ed.

Later, as he guzzled down another beer, Bechter had another question for Henderson.

"Hey buddy, you notice something?"

"What's that?" asked Ed.

"Here we are in the fifth inning and we ain't seen one fight. Not one. What's up with that?"

Henderson smiled and simply said, "We never see fights here. People just show up and enjoy the game."

Bechter simply shook his head in disbelief.

A couple of innings later the obnoxious fan was denied a beer.

"Sorry sir, you've had enough already," said the vender.

"What the hell is going on here?" moaned the agitated Bechter. "This is ridiculous. You people sit here like y'all civilized or something. There ain't no fighting, no heckling the other team, nobody's drunk, everyone is smiling and having a good old time. Well now, ain't that (bleeping) peachy? I can't believe this. This is the worst game I ever went to. You people suck. I ain't coming back to this place. Screw y'all!"

"Sir, can I ask you a question?" said Ed.

"What?" snapped Bechter.

"Where ya from?"

"Philadelphia. Why?"

There were no further questions.

THERE USED TO BE A TENEMENT RIGHT HERE

The elderly gentleman stared quietly at the baseball stadium. He couldn't believe his eyes or hide his sadness.

"I can't understand why they would tear down a perfectly good housing tenement and replace it with a ballpark," said a somber Gil Bedford. "All the memories gone forever. For no good reason."

While many claim the ballpark enhances the city neighborhood, Bedford disagrees.

"I grew up in the McKeever Apartments. My childhood is gone with my building. I can't show my kids or grandkids where I lived for the first 32 years of my life. I'll never be able to show them my apartment that had no heat in the winter," Bedford said as a tear rolled down his cheek. "I won't be able to share with them the leaky faucets in the bathroom or the cockroaches scurrying along in the kitchen. We won't be able to walk the fourteen flights of stairs to get to the apartment because the elevator was broken. I'll never forget the fun and games we had dodging the rats running wild in the hallways and stairwells. I remember the time, I must have been twelve, when I found a dead body on the roof. It was my first introduction to chalk outlines. And now it's all gone. Gone for a stupid baseball stadium."

21 COPIES SOLD!

Everything he wrote turned to gold. Yes, Mike Vaccaro of the New York Post, the premier sports columnist in America, worked his magic every time he tapped on the keyboard.

People across the country would faithfully read his newspaper columns.

His books, "1941—The Greatest Year in Sports," "Emperors and Idiots," and "The First Fall Classic" were highly acclaimed and well received.

If Vaccaro wrote it, people wanted to read it.

That's why Vaccaro was stunned when his latest book didn't fare so well. Apparently the public just wasn't ready for, "Fitness Tips From Sports Writers."

MANNY BEING MOMMY

While taking fertility drugs may have landed Dodgers outfielder Manny Ramirez in hot water with Major League Baseball, it has certainly paid off for the slugger.

In December, Ramirez gave birth to a beautiful, healthy, dreadlock-headed, eight pound, five ounce baby girl.

"I don't know why I was suspended for taking performance enhancing drugs," said Ramirez. "How does taking female fertility drugs enhance your baseball performance?"

Ramirez was suspended fifty games for taking the fertility drug, Human Chorionic Gonadotropin.

"I hated to miss fifty games," Ramirez explained.

"But I wanted to have a child, so the suspension was worth it to have a beautiful baby girl."

The baby, named Manuelita Pedroia Ramirez, is doing well. Mom meanwhile is getting ready for spring training.

RETAIL BATTLE

Former NHL enforcer Tie Domi received just a warning after getting into an altercation with a rival mall worker.

Domi, following a lengthy NHL career, began a new occupation in the exciting world of retail. He was working at Abercrombie and Fitch at the Bayview Village Mall in Toronto when a worker from The Gap strolled into the store. A&F Manager Sean Patterson explains what happened next.

"Tie was folding some shirts when this guy from The Gap walked in. I think he made a crack to Tie about his folding techniques which sent Tie into a rage. He pulled this guy's shirt over his head and proceeded to beat him senseless," Patterson stated. "To be fair to Tie, it wasn't explained to him that what he did playing hockey doesn't translate into the real world."

"I didn't know I couldn't take matters into my own hands," said Domi. "I mean, I spent twenty years punching people's lights out in hockey. For me it's second nature. Who knew you couldn't do that off the ice? Seriously, who knew? I mean, the guy asked for it when he said he wasn't surprised to see a former Maple Leaf still folding."

The entire episode has left Keith Wilkers bitter. "I lost my job and my teeth for simply walking into a rival store. I actually wanted to fill out an application because I was tired of working with the idiots at The Gap. Then this Domi moron jumps me. He gets a slap on the wrist from mall security, then a promotion for the publicity he generated for the store. I get fired and a liquid diet for six weeks. And I'm the bad guy? Man, life in retail is a tough deal."

AN UNDERSTANDING DAD

Doug knew it would be a very difficult discussion. His dad was a star quarterback for Lamkin High and lived for high school football. Pops still liked to relive his glory years for the Lambs. Now he had to tell his father that he was kicked off the team.

"Dad," Doug said softly and with much trepidation, "I'm not on the team anymore."

His father, Phil, was not happy. "This is your senior year. You can't quit."

"I didn't quit Dad. I, um …I got kicked off the team."

"What? Uh, you're not some kind-of homo are you?"

"No Dad, no."

"What the hell then? I'm going to the school now and give that candy-ass coach a piece of my mind. This is unacceptable."

"No Dad, don't do that. I don't belong on the team."

"What are you talking about?"

"Dad, I'm, uh, I don't know how to say this, but, um, Dad, I'm hooked on meth."

Phil paused for a few moments. He took a closer look at his son who was fighting back the tears.

"Son, it's alright. It's okay. I know most kids who are hooked on math aren't good football players. Not everyone can be a star and big man on campus like I was. Hey, you'll probably have a better shot at life being hooked on math than hooked on football. Look at me son. Math would have helped me. But no, here I am a former football hero and legend in this town and I work in the nursery department at Home Depot. Son, don't worry about football. Hit those math books the way I used to hit receivers on the post pattern."

"No Dad, meth. I'm hooked on meth."

"I know son and I'm alright with it."

Dad looked closely at his son. He was about to give him a hug. Then he was startled. "Oh my God, what's with your face? All those open sores on your face. And your teeth! They're black and falling out. Holy crap Doug, look at your face, you're a mess. No wonder you got kicked off the team!"

SHOOTING AVERTED

"So what brings you to New Orleans?" the waitress asked the visitor sitting at the counter.

"I'm going to the Saints game tomorrow," replied Dave Kelley.

"Nice. You must be excited," the waitress said.

"Not really, I have a job to do," Kelley said matter-of-factly.

"What job is that?"

"I have to shoot Drew Brees."

Immediately, two burly off-duty police officers eavesdropping on the conversation jumped Kelley, taking him to the ground and cuffing him.

Never before had the long-time Sports Illustrated photographer been treated so harshly.

OZZIE CLEANS IT UP

Chicago media members were concerned following a recent press gathering with White Sox Manager Ozzie Guillen, in the team dugout before last night's game.

Team broadcaster Ken "Hawk" Harrelson said, "After we finished talking to Ozzie one writer pointed out that Oz didn't use any obscenities during the twenty minute session. None. This from a guy who was cussing and swearing the day he exited the womb."

A concerned writer, Rick Telander said, "Ozzie and I have had our differences, but when I asked him why the team was underachieving he gave me a reasoned thoughtful answer instead of telling me to go (bleep) myself. I'm worried. What happened to the real Ozzie?"

"I hope Ozzie is alright," noted sports talker Carmen DeFalco. "He actually used words such as—sanctimonious, obtuse, and exponentially. We're thinking of some type of intervention. I mean, what will we talk about if Ozzie doesn't flip out on a daily basis?"

When out of town broadcaster Josh Lewin was selected to approach Guillen in his office to see what was going on, Ozzie said, "I didn't use bad language so I could win a bet. Now get your ass out of here, you …"

For the next five minutes Lewin was the target of a vintage, obscenity laced Ozzie Guillen tirade.

Lewin happily alerted the Chicago media, "Don't worry guys. Ozzie is back. Thank goodness."

SLASHING THE NIGHT AWAY

Kevin Haney's competitive hockey days were behind him but the 33-year-old estate broker thought it would be fun to get back on the ice in an adult non-checking league.

"I felt the urge to play again and the exercise would do me good," reasoned Kevin.

A forward, Kevin had a blast in his first game, plus his team won! It was more fun than he thought. He was a little sore the next few days but it was the good kind of sore. He was looking forward to the next game the following week.

During the first period of the second game, Kevin parked himself in front of the net hoping to screen the goaltender.

Whack!

The goalie slashed Kevin in the back of the calf. He fell to the ice in pain. No penalty was called.

As the game progressed, Kevin was tripped up skating in front of the goalie and also got punched in the back of the head by the feisty netminder.

"Every time I got assaulted by the goalie the referee was looking away. It was frustrating," recalled Haney.

In the third period he finally snapped. While skating in front of the goal, Kevin was slashed in the ankle, again by the sneaky goalie. That was it as far as Kevin was concerned. He pulled himself off the ice and attacked the aggressive goaltender. Punches flew and an all-out brawl ensued.

Kevin was given a two minute roughing penalty, a two minute unsportsmanlike conduct penalty, a five minute major for fighting, a game misconduct and was suspended by the league for five games.

As for the goalie, she, yes she, didn't receive any penalties or injuries. But she did hand out a black eye, a fat lip and a bloody nose which Kevin was tendering to in the locker room.

After the game, several teammates looked at Kevin with disgust. Finally, one teammate, Angelo Ricci, approached Haney and said, "Dude, you got beat up by girl. What the hell were you thinking? Amber's the nicest player in the league. She's a sweetheart."

THE OUTCAST

The Bethel Park barber shop was crowded as usual on a Monday morning. The locals were still excited over the previous day's Steelers playoff win.

George, who was the oldest fan in the group, said "That was the greatest game I ever saw. The Patriots had that game in the bag and we took it away from them."

"It was a great game, no question," countered Fritz, "But the best ever?"

Immediately the debate was on. It got pretty raucous at times, but the fellas enjoyed each other's company and looked forward to the AFC title game against the Colts.

Finally Wally walked into the room, later than usual.

"Hey Wally, about time you got here," yelled Sammy above the chatter. "Was yesterday's game the greatest ever?"

Wally hesitated and then said, "Man, I'm glad we won. I heard it was a great game."

The room went silent. Mouths were agape.

"Wally, let me get this straight," George began. "You didn't see the game?"

Wally looked around the quiet room. He was a little nervous.

All eyes were fixed upon him.

"Well, Hazel dragged me to the mall. We had to get a few things and she wanted to spend some time together. You can all relate guys, right?"

The dozen or so men in the room were stunned.

A few gently shook their heads from side to side.

George broke the awkward silence.

"Wally, I think you better go now."

While he may have thought he was doing the right thing when he took his crabby wife to the shopping mall during a Steelers playoff game, it was certainly a costly outing for Wally; an outing he would never live down.

AN EXTREME ENDORSEMENT

The Orthopedics Association of America has given it's full support and endorsement to both the summer and winter X-Games.

"While some find these extreme sports dangerous," began Dr. Andrew Scheckman, at the yearly convention, "The OAA feels they are wholesome sports and that more people, of all ages, should participate."

When asked if his three children are involved in sports such as aerial skiing, skateboarding tricks or bike stunts, Dr. Scheckman said, "Are you kidding me? No way. You can get seriously hurt doing that non-sense."

Since extreme sports have come to the mainstream via ESPN's coverage and the influx of skate parks in cities across the country, visits to orthopedic surgeons have increased six-hundred ninety-one percent since 2001.

The OAA also endorses hang-gliding, ski jumping, sky diving, mountain climbing, alligator wrestling and husbands refusing to go shopping with their wives during football season.

FLAGGED

Melissa Page was excited when she got the news that she was hired by a San Diego law firm as a secretary and personal assistant to attorney Ed Hochuli.

First and foremost, she now had a job after being unemployed for six months. Plus, she got to work for Mr. Hochuli who, beside his reputation for being a great boss, was also an NFL referee and Melissa enjoyed football.

"I was told that Mr. Hochuli was demanding but fair to work for," Melissa recalls. "But I didn't realize when I came aboard that he brought a referee mentality to the office."

Hochuli, a veteran NFL ref, frequently roams the office pointing out transgressions by the staff, but he doesn't stop there.

"Instead of a suit and tie like most lawyers, Eddie walks around in a black and white referee shirt," said law partner Peter Robson. "Of course the shirt is extra tight to show off the guns. Anyway, he'll blow his whistle and throw a flag. That's right he throws penalty flags around the office when he sees things he finds fault with."

"My first day on the job Mr. Hochuli flagged me for not rinsing out my coffee cup to his satisfaction," said Melissa. "He blew his whistle, threw the flag at my feet then got on the intercom and said, 'We've got improper rinsing of a drinking apparatus on Ms. Page. This is a five minute infraction."

Since Hochuli can't penalize workers yards, he punishes them with minutes.

"I get off work at 5," said Melissa. "Mr. Hochuli made me stay over. It was 5:05 before I could leave."

Ken Briggston, a junior partner, recalls one day when he was hit with a whopping forty-five minutes in penalties. "Yeah, I got fifteen minutes for a personal foul when I turned the corner with my head down and walked into Jerry the mail guy. I got another fifteen minutes for unsportsmanlike conduct when I argued about it with Ed. Won't do that again. And then, around 4:30 I got popped for delay of work, spending too much time in the bathroom. That was another fifteen minutes. I was supposed to leave at 6, but ended up leaving at 6:45. Wouldn't have been so bad, but I was late picking my wife up from the airport."

Amanda Leonard from accounting was angry when Hochuli penalized her last week. "Tuesday morning I was making a copy of my dad's death certificate and he came in and got me for 'Illegal use of the copy machine.' He even threw in the hand signals for that one. I'll be honest with you. I wanted to shove that flag and whistle up his ass."

Senior partner Alex Hanigraff recalls the time he got kicked out of the office for a day. "I was flirting with one of the snappy interns from San Diego State and Ed saw me. He threw a flag for illegal touching and work day misconduct and tossed me out of the office for two days. But I never initiated the hug, she did. I threw a red flag to review the call and the video monitor in the hall proved beyond a reasonable doubt that she initiated the hug. So Ed got back on the intercom and said, 'After further review, the penalty will be a work day ejection for today only and not tomorrow.'"

Hochuli says that he rules the office with an iron fist because he wants things to "run efficiently and to keep the staff on their toes." It also helps keep him sharp for Sundays in the fall when he has to preside over NFL contests. Of course, despite his apparent love of discipline, he still blew a crucial call in last year's Chargers-Broncos game.

"That's right," said Melissa. "But I have to give him credit. He threw a flag on himself the next day in the office. Yep, Mr. Hochuli is a wack job, but he's our wack job."

Immediately after uttering those words, Ms. Page was startled by a shrieking whistle and the sight of a buffed up referee in the doorway throwing a yellow flag at her and reaching for the intercom. She would be, once again, staying past 5.

Acknowledgements

This is the portion of the book where I thank people. The reason that is important is because the support and friendship given to me by the following people is something I don't take for granted and helps motivate and inspire me. So, thanks for your friendship, feedback and all the crap you give me too.

First and foremost I have to thank my wife Gwyn, who also happens to be my best friend ever.

Thanks to publisher Linda L. Young. Without all her hard work and encouragement there probably wouldn't be another Turf Tales book. So, if you don't like the book, blame Linda.

Of course I must thank the Turf crew. Artificial Turf has been on the air since February of 2003 and the reason I still love doing the show is because of Andy Cornell, the most positive person I know, along with Casey Bloyer, Justin Adams, Brett Davis and Ed Henderson. I'd also like to thank Kevin Wheeler of KMOX radio in St. Louis—for my money the best sports talk show host in America.

My friends at Primerica Financial Services are some of the best people I've ever been around, period. Coach Cornell, along with his lovely wife Anne, Derek and Brittany Chambers, James and Ashley Lamkin, Chris Reed and Loke Kalili, Malia Kalili, Jeff Moody and Dawn Estenor, Ryan Moody, Jade Wicks, Brian and Renee Rice, Sean Patterson, Barb The Bulldog and Frank Sayers and, of course, the impressive and incomparable Mark and Cathy Marchesani who put this fine, winning team together. Contrary to rumors, Mark is not a professional bowler but he does play a mean banjo.

I'd also like to thank, from KNUS radio, Tom Moller, Nia Bender, Cliff Powers, Roberto (Bobby) Nunez, Chris Carroll, Cliff Mikkelson, Derek Jackson, Kelly Michaels and Brian Taylor. Kelly and Brian green lighted Artificial Turf way back when and have allowed it to stay on the air; which means they probably don't listen to the program.

At KCCB-TV Channel 8 I have to thank my former color commentator Ryan Kloberdanz, my stat man supreme and former Turf producer Don Pablo Apodaca, Victor Sieff and Kim Greason.

My baseball teammates in the Denver Over-35 league: John Namovicz, Scott Blaise, Mike Carsella, John Castellano, Jim O'Connor, Ted "Professional Hitter" Stavish, Rob Watkins, Chris Cruz, Dave "King" Kelley, Chad Lucero, Jeremy Weiss, Joe Hannon and Paul Harris.

Thanks to the www.turfsports.net website contributors and friends, Tiffany Morgan, Marty Lenz, Tony Jarboe, John Higgins and all of the voters on our Turf Top 17 College Football Poll.

And thanks to Rick Schultz, Kent Calhoun, Marty Higgins, Mike Vaccaro, Barry Steckel, Mike Erdek, John Feinstein, Jan Sumner, Freddie Coleman, Dave Itchkawitz, Ed and Julie Gutierrez, Jimmy Harrison, Billy Thornton, Gary Casey, David Brody, Jon Chelesnik, Jeff Andrews, Jim Roser, Terry Cuff, Amber Marcelli, Nick Vella, Mark Knudson, Tim and Kristina McLaughlin and the families McGurgan, Jarboe and Gantter as well Nick Nicoletti, my sister Mary, and her great kids Chelsea and Collin.

Also, I'd like to thank Mark Kinsey from The Denver Sports Column, where I had the book launch party and where Tom Moller and I filmed the internet commercial for More Turf Tales.

If I forgot someone, my bad.

Lastly, I'd like to thank Jeets, the greatest cat on the planet.

Coming soon the second edition of Bill Rogan's book, *A Renegade Summer ...A Look Back On The Hudson Valley Renegades' Inaugural Season.*

This baseball classic will take you inside life in the minor leagues, as seen through the eyes of their radio broadcaster, and will feature an update on the cast of characters that made the 1994 Renegades such a special and memorable team.

Look for this and other great books at:
www.maxq4u.com.
MaxQ Enterprises
A Rocky Mountain Publisher